Intent to Kill

Also by Emma Page:

INTENT TO KILL

Emma Page

Constable • London

First published in Great Britain 1998
by Constable & Company Ltd
3 The Lanchesters, 162 Fulham Palace Road
London W6 9ER
Copyright © 1998 Emma Page
The right of Emma Page to be
identified as the author of this work
has been asserted by her in accordance
with the Copyright, Designs and Patents Act 1988
ISBN 0 09 478670 4
Set in Palatino 10pt by
Pure Tech India Ltd, Pondicherry
Printed and bound in Great Britain by
MPG Books Ltd, Bodmin, Cornwall

A CIP catalogue record for this book
is available from The British Library

For Christopher
with much love
as always

1

Paragon Tools occupied a prime site on the Cannonbridge industrial estate. At a minute or two after five on a sunny Monday evening in late September, Ted Gilchrist left the main building and walked across to the bicycle shed in the corner of the carpark. He was an agile, wiry little man in his mid-fifties, mild-mannered and amenable. He had worked in the Paragon accounts office for the whole of the thirty-odd years the firm had been in existence.

Paragon had started out from modest beginnings on the other side of town, moving after ten years to its present purpose-built premises. The firm had ridden out the recession and was doing better than ever now, at home and abroad. It had never been floated on the Stock Exchange but remained entirely owned by the man who had founded it and still ran it.

Ted Gilchrist had always worked with unremitting application, never missing a day, finally rising, seven years ago, to the post of chief accountant. Today he had worked even harder than usual as his number two, Matthew Shardlow, was currently on leave; he had left on Saturday for two weeks in Majorca.

Ted set off on his bicycle for his cottage on the edge of town, the cottage he had lived in all his married life. His daughter, his only child, lived in a nearby semi with her husband and their six-year-old son, Andrew. His daughter worked part-time in an office; her husband, an amiable, easy-going man, was a musician, out of work as often as not.

Ted was not unacquainted with money worries himself. He had just about paid off his mortgage, twelve months after his promotion to chief accountant, when his mother-in-law's health began to fail and it became clear that she wouldn't be able to live alone for much longer. She was a widow, always hypercritical and demanding, awash now with self-pity. His wife had found it difficult enough to get on with her before and couldn't even begin to contemplate having her to live with them. 'She'll have to go into a home,' she told Ted in a tone he knew of old, a tone that brooked no argument.

Not any old home, of course; it had to be one of the best available locally, or she would never agree to enter its doors. Ted had viewed the proposal with deep misgiving. Such homes didn't come cheap and he would be called on to fund the difference between the charges and what his mother-in-law could afford. It would be no mean sum every month and there was no telling how long she might live.

But his misgivings were brushed aside and in due course his mother-in-law went into a home, after a good deal of noisy weeping on her part, accusations of heartlessness. That was five and a half years ago and she was still alive. The home looked after her with every care and she had settled in well. She was in better health now than when she had first gone there; she looked as if she could soldier on for a good few years yet.

Ted's route home took him along leafy avenues, through a suburb of large old houses, all now turned into flats, guesthouses, kindergartens, doctors' surgeries. When he reached the fringe of the suburb he looked ahead with proprietorial pride and pleasure at one particularly large, handsome building, Elmgrove House, now a private prep school standing in extensive grounds. On his daily rides along this route over the years, Elmgrove House had always taken his eye. What a start in life it would give a child to attend a school like that; it enjoyed a first-class reputation.

Ted had come up the hard way, with no advantages of birth or money. His qualifications had been laboriously gained at evening classes. Ever since the birth of his grandson he had yearned for something better for the boy, something to make his path through life easier. Andrew was bright; Ted had seen that from the start. If only he could scrape together the money to send him to Elmgrove House. But it seemed a vain aspiration. And Elmgrove House would be only the beginning of it; there would be the next school up the ladder and then a university. Ted's wife couldn't see the necessity for private education; Ted had got on well enough without it. She certainly wouldn't agree to her mother being moved to a less expensive home in order to build up a fund to pay the boy's fees.

But Ted's dream had at last materialized. A surge of happiness rose in his breast, as always these days, when he neared Elmgrove House. Twelve months ago Andrew had put on his smart new uniform for his first day at the school. He had shown no nervousness but had settled in at once and made friends; he jumped out of bed every morning in joyful expectation of the day ahead.

As Ted rode past the school he let his gaze rove fondly over the building and the grounds. He turned his head to snatch a last backward glance. A car came swiftly out of a side road, the driver in haste to catch a train. He glimpsed the bicycle too late, he struck it smack on, sending Ted flying up into the air and down again on to the road, fracturing his skull, breaking his neck, killing him instantly.

Later the same evening, on the outskirts of a town forty-five miles from Cannonbridge, in the office of his woodturning business, an enterprise of no great size, Stephen Hibberd and his wife Nell sat frowning over the books. The handful of men employed in the business had all gone home at the usual time; there was no urgent order to keep them working after hours, nor had there been such an order for some time. None of the men would have been surprised to learn that the boss and his wife were staying late, racking their brains to try to find some way of drumming up orders in the next few weeks. Every man jack of them was well aware that if nothing substantial turned up soon they would all be out of a job by Christmas.

Stephen scribbled down figures, contemplated them, crossed them out, scribbled down a fresh set, another and another. He uttered a long despairing groan. No way he could get the figures to come out in any sort of encouraging fashion. He felt anxiety claw at his guts. He and Nell stood to lose not only the business but the house as well; they had had to put that up as security for the bank loan.

Stephen was twenty-eight years old, with a face that was always serious and these days wore an anxious frown. His wife was one year younger, pretty enough, trim and competent-looking, with an air of shrewd common sense. They had known each other since their schooldays.

Stephen had been a foundling, left at the door of a local hospital at a few days old. He had gone from one foster-home to another, some good, some less good, then to a children's home where he stayed till he left school at sixteen.

Nell was an only child; her father had run a one-man woodturning business from outbuildings in the garden of his cottage. As a schoolboy Stephen had gone round to help him in the evenings and at weekends, making himself so useful that when he left school Nell's father had taken him on full-time; Stephen had found digs nearby. Times were good and the business prospered. Nell took a secretarial course after leaving school and found herself a job in the office of a factory a short bus-ride from home.

When Stephen was nineteen the young couple married. At eighteen Nell had come into a very useful sum of money under the will of her grandmother and she put the whole of it towards the cost of a small house close to her parents. By way of a wedding present her father provided another substantial sum towards the purchase; for the remainder Stephen took out a mortgage.

Not long after the wedding Nell's father learned that he was suffering from terminal cancer. During the last months of his life Stephen ran the business more or less single-handed. After her father's death Nell left her factory job and in partnership with Stephen took over the woodturning business, agreeing to pay her mother a fair share of the profits for the rest of her life. Her mother was an accommodating woman, good-natured and supportive. When in due course grandchildren were born, a boy, followed two years later by a girl, she was only too happy to help in any way she could, freeing Nell to continue playing a full part in the running of the business.

Trade in general was excellent, order-books full. Stephen began to think of expansion and within a few months of taking over he saw a golden opportunity. A commercial garage had been put out of business by the opening of a bypass and Stephen was able to raise a bank loan to buy the premises at a knock-down price. The garage workshop was speedily converted, woodworking machinery installed. Things went swimmingly for a time and then, imperceptibly at first but slowly gathering pace, came the downturn.

'We could try Paragon Tools,' Nell exclaimed now with sudden inspiration.

'Paragon?' Stephen echoed on a ruminative note. He hadn't so far approached Paragon which was outside their normal forty-mile radius and was larger than the usual run of firms they supplied. But it was certainly a thought. Paragon would have a constant demand for handles for all types of tools; he could supply them in any wood, any shape and size, any finish. If he cut prices to the bone he might be in with a chance. His expression lightened, he looked almost cheerful. 'We'll do it!' he decided, sitting back in his chair. 'We'll do it right away!'

2

In the middle of Friday afternoon Robert Anstey, the sole owner of Paragon Tools, sat at his desk in his office, opposite Stephen Hibberd, at the close of their talk. Anstey was sixty-two, tall, of athletic build. He had kept his figure and had only a light sprinkling of grey in his thick, dark hair. Still straight of back and easy of movement, he was able to look upon himself as no more than middle-aged. His habitual expression was somewhat austere.

But his manner was cordial enough as he handed back the samples Hibberd had brought and gave his decision. The samples and prices were eminently satisfactory, as good as those of any other supplier. But there was at present no vacancy for another supplier on his list. 'I'll certainly be in touch if an opening does arise,' he assured Hibberd. Openings did arise from time to time, sometimes in recent years with surprising suddenness when some small firm went abruptly down for good.

He walked with Hibberd to the door and stepped out into the corridor with him, still chatting genially. He had taken a liking to Hibberd who came across as ambitious and hardworking, a man who could be expected to adhere scrupulously to the terms of a contract – something to which Anstey attached the greatest importance. A stickler in all such matters himself, he would overlook no negligence in others. He had been pleased to note that Hibberd had arrived in good time for his appointment. Had he turned up late, whatever his excuse, that would have put

11

paid to any chance of his name ever being added to the list of suppliers.

Anstey was a self-made man and could well sympathize with Hibberd in his efforts to get on; he had known some exceedingly hairy moments in his own early days. He recognized the look of deep-seated anxiety in Hibberd's eyes, try as Hibberd might to appear relaxed and confident. There had been times enough in the mornings of those early days when Anstey had seen that selfsame look gaze back at him from his shaving mirror.

As they stood talking in the doorway, a young man, Ian Bryant, rounded the bend in the corridor several yards away, coming to a halt at the sight of the two men. He was a temporary employee of Paragon, twenty-eight years old, tall and strongly built. He withdrew far enough to be almost out of view himself while still being able to keep his eye on them.

A couple of minutes later the two men shook hands and Hibberd went off along the corridor and down the stairs towards the exit, frowning as he went, trying to decide if Anstey was merely being polite or if there was any real chance of getting on to the list. Anstey had seemed genuinely interested and helpful and he didn't appear to be a man who would buoy someone up with delusive hope – but then again he probably wouldn't want to cast someone down for want of an encouraging word.

As soon as Anstey had gone back into his office Ian Bryant moved to a corridor window. He stood looking out, watching as Hibberd crossed the car-park and got into a van. He was able to read without difficulty the name and address on the side of the van.

Back in his office, Robert Anstey didn't immediately return to his desk. He remained motionless for several moments, assailed by another of the odd turns that had begun to plague him. A surge of fatigue rose inside him. He closed his eyes and let it wash over him, ebb away again. All his life he had enjoyed good health but three or four months ago he had begun to experience a curious assortment of sensations. A good holiday is what's needed, he had told himself. He had taken his usual summer break in the certainty of coming back to work invigorated and refreshed. But he had been back at work for only a couple of weeks and already the unpleasant symptoms were starting up again.

He went back to his desk and sat down. A little more exercise and relaxation might do the trick, he'd better begin taking one or two afternoons a week off to play golf. Lilian wouldn't mind putting in some extra time to cover for him. She was always ready to take on more responsibility, she would do anything to help him. Lilian was his second wife; it had been a second marriage for both of them. He had long been a widower and Lilian had been widowed a few years. She had been Robert's personal assistant for two years before their marriage four years ago and she still put in three or four mornings a week at Paragon, with an occasional afternoon if she was needed. Robert found her sharp intelligence, her business acumen and general shrewdness invaluable assets.

But he would say nothing to her about the fatigue or the other symptoms. She would urge him to seek medical advice and he'd never been one to go running to the doctor every five minutes. All that did was to blow up every minor ailment into an importance it didn't warrant. He was a firm believer in a sensible way of life, applying intelligence to one's situation. He had always risen early, was always at his desk by seven thirty, but he had taken care, nevertheless, not to overwork. He had never made a practice of staying late at the office. He had always walked, always taken a certain minimum of exercise, watched what he ate, neither smoked nor drank.

He had a shrewd notion of what Dr Thornley would say if he did visit him: at sixty-two you must expect some signs of wear and tear. He grimaced at the notion, so foreign to his whole outlook. He was repelled by the very thought of old age and had so far refused even to countenance it. It had always been his aim to go on working until he dropped and he had no intention now of departing from his plan. That was one of the most valuable perks of being your own boss: no one could tell you when to pack up and go.

He became suddenly aware that the fatigue had passed, he felt perfectly all right again. Yes, he told himself with resolute confidence, a little more relaxation, a little more exercise, and I'll be back in top form before Christmas.

Ian Bryant was able to catch Anstey's secretary, a middle-aged spinster with whom he was on chatty terms, as she left her office at the end of the day. Before many minutes had passed he had learned the purpose of Stephen Hibberd's visit to Paragon and how Hibberd had fared.

As he parted company with the secretary, another woman, Delphine Tate, came out of a nearby office. She was much younger than the secretary, considerably better-looking and more fashionably dressed. She worked partly in the general office and partly for Mrs Anstey, acting as her secretary on the mornings she came in. At the sight of Ian she quickened her pace, catching up with him as he went off towards the stairs.

'Hello, there,' she said. He stopped, turned his head and looked back at her. She gazed at him with frank appreciation. He was certainly well built but his style of looks wasn't the kind she usually went for; she normally liked something a good deal more eye-catching. She couldn't put her finger on what it was about him that got to her. She had felt it the first time she laid eyes on him, in early June. She had got back from holiday to discover that Ian had been taken on out of the blue, in her absence. She had lost no time in chatting him up but had had no success whatever. And yet she was sure he fancied her; she could always tell. At twenty-three she was no novice in such matters and she had never believed in waiting for the male to make the first move. She had invited him to various get-togethers during the summer: a barbecue, a party, a jazz evening. But it invariably appeared that he'd already made other arrangements. She wasn't accustomed to being turned down, however pleasantly; she didn't give up that easily.

Now she tried a different, if more corny, tack: she'd been given two theatre tickets for tomorrow evening. Would Ian like to see the show? She'd heard it was first-class. But again he smiled and shook his head. Again he thanked her, again he told her with his customary good manners that he was sorry, he'd made other plans.

She stood looking after him as he went off down the stairs. She knew from a friend in Personnel that Ian wasn't married, wasn't divorced or separated. And she was willing to bet every last penny that he wasn't gay. If he already had a steady girlfriend, why not come straight out and say so?

I haven't finished with you yet, my lad, she said to herself as he vanished round a curve in the stairs; I'll have you one of these days.

3

The weather continued mild and dry; Sunday was a calmly golden day. In her immaculate semi, a short bus-ride from where the Ansteys lived, Hester Whiting, their daily cook-house-keeper, had just about managed to find enough little jobs, indoors and out, to occupy her time until she could get ready to set off for Kincraig, the Ansteys' house, immediately after lunch.

She was forty years old and looked every day of her age. She was slightly built, of nondescript appearance, without a trace of make-up. Her longish mousy hair was taken up on top of her head in a straggly knot. She was dowdily dressed, with not so much as a passing nod to current fashion. But her features were good, her eyes large and well set, the colour of amber; a different way of dressing would show her figure to advantage.

A widow for some six months, living on her own, she had to make an unremitting effort to avoid low spirits. It wasn't too bad, Monday to Friday, when she spent the greater part of her day at Kincraig, working from nine to one fifteen and four thirty to seven. Mrs Anstey was often there and a woman came in twice a week to do the rough cleaning. Liggitt, the gardener-handyman, was always about the place. But Saturdays and Sundays were a different matter. There was a limit to how far her own housework, gardening and shopping could be made to stretch, how much television could be watched, how much radio listened to, how many library books read.

She had never been on sociable terms with the neighbours, never had the gift of easy friendship. When her husband was alive the days had been full enough. Gilbert Whiting had been thirty years her senior, zealous in the activities of the local chapel. Though never a wholehearted believer herself, she had been brought up to attend the same chapel and felt it her duty to support her husband. She had baked cakes for fund-raising fairs and bazaars, served on jumble-sale stalls, provided refreshments for meetings held in the house.

Gilbert was a childless widower when she married him. A tight-fisted man of narrow views and settled habits, censorious and demanding, his meals had to be cooked the way his first wife – and before her, his mother – had cooked them, his shirts laundered the way those two women had laundered them, the housework done according to their exacting standards.

All this Hester had accepted unquestioningly as part of the normal scheme of things. Her father had been much the same sort of man and her mother had never by word or look displayed the smallest sign of irritation or resentment at her lot. Hester was an only child, born late in the marriage. Her father had been an assistant in a men's outfitter's; they lived in a council house. Her mother had fallen ill during Hester's last year at school; she had died at the end of the summer term. There was no question of Hester taking a job or any form of training. Her path was made immediately and abundantly clear to her: she was to stay at home, run the house, look after her father. She never dreamed of rebelling; indeed, she had felt considerable pride at being entrusted with such adult responsibility.

Gilbert Whiting and her father knew each other from chapel. When Hester was twenty-three, with her father in rapidly failing health, Gilbert began to call round more often and it became plain that he was courting Hester. He talked over the question of marriage with her father before speaking of it to Hester. 'I'd strongly advise you to take him after I've gone,' her father counselled her. All he had to leave her was some modest savings. 'Gilbert has his own house, a decent job' – Gilbert was a senior clerk in the offices of the local electricity board – 'and he'll have a good pension when he retires.' Her father didn't find it necessary to spell out two further points: there had never been any other candidates for her hand and Gilbert was likely to die many years before Hester who would not only inherit the house and her husband's savings but would also, as Gilbert's widow, come in for a very nice pension from the electricity board.

This reasoning struck Hester as eminently sound and not long after her father's death she married Gilbert in a quiet ceremony at the chapel. That was seventeen years ago. The marriage hadn't produced children, any more than Gilbert's first marriage had done. Hester would have liked children but hadn't in the circumstances permitted herself to entertain any great hopes of motherhood. The matter was never discussed between them and it was unthinkable that she should speak of it to a doctor.

Her father's view of her future had proved to be well founded. She certainly had no need to go out to work after her husband's death. She not only had the house and the pension but Gilbert's savings had turned out to be a good deal more substantial than she would ever have guessed. All in all, she felt herself very comfortably off indeed. She had never acquired extravagant tastes, had never had a foreign holiday, never learned to drive a car.

It had taken all the nerve she possessed, after Gilbert's death, to stop going to chapel, to resist the none too subtle pressures on her to continue to attend, but resist she did. One drawback of this change in her life was that it deprived her of her social contacts and another drawback was the way it left her at a particularly loose end on a Sunday, previously a purposeful, well-structured day.

She tried taking classes in cookery and flower-arranging but found they lacked the most essential ingredient: purpose. To what end, she asked herself, was she seeking to improve her proficiency in these skills?

The solution to her difficulties stared her in the face: she must find a job. It would alleviate her loneliness, provide her with a purpose. But she struggled against it. She had never in her life had a single day's paid employment and the notion terrified her. But it came down at last to a straightforward choice: master her fears or slide into depression. She chose to master her fears.

It would have to be some sort of domestic post, it was all she knew. She counted herself very fortunate in landing the job at Kincraig. The Ansteys' resident housekeeper was retiring and they had decided to replace her with someone coming in daily. It was all working out most satisfactorily. The Ansteys treated her with kindness and consideration; the wages were excellent, the work varied and interesting, well within her capacity.

By one fifteen this Sunday she had eaten the snack lunch which was all she could be bothered to produce for herself. It didn't take many minutes to clear away and wash up. She would walk round to Kincraig. It was a beautiful day and the bus

17

service was sketchy on a Sunday. Walking had the added advantage of using up a little more time; she didn't want to arrive too early. She would have been happy to work at Kincraig every Saturday and Sunday and regularly dropped a hint to this effect. But the Ansteys were anxious not to exploit her readiness to oblige and she had so far managed to put in only an occasional Sunday afternoon when, as today, visitors were expected.

Today it was the Farrells, relatives of Mr Anstey, who were coming to tea. A youngish couple, pleasant enough; not long married, it appeared. They lived in Wychford, a town ten miles from Cannonbridge, and had been to Sunday tea twice before since Hester had started working for the Ansteys.

She let herself out into the sunny afternoon and set off at an easy pace for Kincraig. By the time she got there the Ansteys should just about have finished lunch. She would clear the table and wash up, have a tidy round in the kitchen. Then she would make a batch of nice little scones – the Farrells had been very complimentary about her scones on their last visit. With the scones seen to she would attend to the flower arrangements – Mrs Anstey was happy to leave them to her. Lay the table, serve the tea. She enjoyed setting an attractive table, she appreciated good table linen, she liked fine china, the look and feel of it. Afterwards, when she had cleared away and washed up, she would see what thoughts Mrs Anstey had about supper. She would carry out any instructions, leave everything ready for the meal, then walk back home the long way round, taking her time. A bite to eat, a look at TV. That took care of the whole of the rest of the day, right up to bedtime. She was feeling almost cheerful by the time she came in sight of the Ansteys' house.

4

Kincraig was a sizeable Victorian villa, a handsome dwelling of local stone, standing in a large, well-kept garden blessed with a good deal of privacy by virtue of tall, clipped hedges, disciplined boundary trees and shrubs.

In the dining-room Robert and Lilian Anstey sat over coffee at the end of an agreeable lunch. Robert's gaze rested with appreciation on his wife; always a pleasure to look at her.

Everything about Lilian, her manner, her way of moving and talking, was quiet and composed. She was thirty-eight years old, with her share of good looks, though in no way striking in appearance. She was above average height, with a slim, supple figure; she had dark hair and a pale, fine skin, luminous grey eyes, widely set. She wore tailored clothes, graceful and unshowy, always suitable, always becoming.

She had no particular liking for cooking or, indeed, for any aspect of housework. She had never learned such skills in her youth and as a young woman before her first marriage, living in a small flat, had managed well enough without them. Both her husbands could afford to employ household help. At the time of her first marriage she had made it her business to acquire the essential minimum of domestic know-how, together with a decent competence in good English cooking. Her first husband, himself a widower, had been, like Robert, a self-made man, and while he had no wish for cordon bleu cookery or other aspects of luxurious living, he did expect a well-run home and appetizing food. When, as today, Lilian produced a meal, it was done, like all she set about, efficiently, with an absence of fuss and disorder, to the satisfaction of those concerned.

The dining-room at Kincraig, like the rest of the house, was comfortably and tastefully furnished, but no more than that; no rare antiques or valuable paintings, no precious porcelain ornaments or costly soft furnishings. Kincraig had belonged to the parents of Robert's first wife, Joan. When he married Joan thirty years ago, he moved into the house from his rented bachelor flat. Joan's parents had been dead a year or two by then; Robert had never known them. The house was furnished now very much as it had been then; he had at no time felt any desire for change. He had no taste for display or pretension, he had risen from a modest background. Lilian had understood all this when she married him and as she had no strong feeling on the subject herself, she had never attempted unnecessary alteration.

They chatted easily, in their customary fashion, over their coffee. Robert's manner, as always, was somewhat detached. He was never outwardly emotional, never accustomed to use endearments, but he loved Lilian and he had loved Joan. He had

19

never been a man for swift, facile attachments, had never, indeed, had a girlfriend before he met Joan. Marriage had always seemed to him a very serious business. He had never seen it as a matter of romance or passion but as a sensible partnership, to be undertaken with a clear head and a judicious assessment of the likely benefits to both parties. One quality above all others had always appeared to him to be the essential foundation for the relationship, of supreme value in the most intimate of all partnerships: the quality of loyalty.

They were just about ready to leave the table when they heard Mrs Whiting let herself in at the side door. Robert took himself off, out into the garden, and Lilian went along to the kitchen to speak to Mrs Whiting before going upstairs to the room she used as a study.

Out in the garden, Robert strolled along the paths in the warm sunshine. He enjoyed a leisurely saunter, listening to the chirruping of the birds, admiring the trees, catching the drift of scents from flowers and shrubs. He found it all immensely relaxing; it allowed him to think things over.

The garden had been laid out years ago, under the direction of Joan's father, and Joan had always taken a keen interest in it. Her parents had employed a gardener but Joan had spent many an hour herself with trowel and hoe. The present gardener, Liggitt, now in his late fifties, had been taken on as a lad straight from school, by Joan's father. Robert had never been a hands-on gardener and after Joan's death he had left the management of the garden to Liggitt, with the general proviso that it should be kept in the main as Joan had known it. Lilian had no greater taste than Robert for personal exertion among the beds and borders and was content, after her marriage, to let things continue in the same way.

There had been no garden for the greater part of Robert's childhood; his widowed mother had had more than enough to do without a garden to look after.

Robert had been an only child and had no more than shadowy memories of his father, who had been a librarian. He had died when Robert was five years old, during a seaside holiday in Dorset. One sunny afternoon, while Robert and his mother made sandcastles, his father had indulged in his hobby of fossil-hunting. A cliff-edge had given way and his father had plunged on to the rocks below. He had died in hospital three days later.

Robert and his mother moved from their spacious semi to a small terrace house. To supplement her modest pension his mother found part-time clerical work. They had just about managed. There was no question of Robert going on to higher education. He left school at the earliest moment and was taken on as an office boy by a local firm of builders' merchants. He worked diligently, studied at evening classes, rising in time to a managerial position. He lived with extreme frugality, saving every penny; he always had it in mind to strike out for himself one day. He kept his eyes ceaselessly open for a niche in the market, watching for the moment of upturn in the national economy.

When he was thirty the firm he worked for became the target of a successful take-over and there were large-scale redundancies. Robert seized his chance, took severance pay, put it with his savings and set up in a small way on his own.

He had timed things well. Eighteen months later, when he met Joan, his little business was flourishing. But his mother was dead by then and he felt himself alone in the world. Six months later he and Joan were married.

Joan was a few years older than her bridegroom and never much favoured in the way of looks, though with an engaging manner and a ready smile. She too had been an only child. Her father had been a master baker, owning a number of shops locally. Joan had come into her inheritance a couple of years before her marriage and occupied herself with good works. On her marriage, entirely of her own free will, she made the whole of her capital available to Robert, who made skilful use of it to expand his business.

They would both have liked children but were never fortunate enough to have any. Joan had no thought of playing any personal part in her husband's business; she was at heart a home-loving woman, unassuming and undemanding. It had been a happy marriage, ending after ten years with the dreadful blow of Joan's death, after a short illness.

It took Robert a long time to get over it. Once again he felt himself alone in the world. He seized the only lifeline he knew: hard work. Things remained like that for fourteen years, when Lilian came to work for him.

By the time of his second marriage he was long reconciled to never having children and in any case considered himself too old by then to think of fatherhood. The matter was never discussed between them. Lilian seemed to have no thoughts of motherhood, so that was that.

Robert halted in his promenading about the garden as a sudden troubling sensation assailed him. He sank on to a nearby seat and remained with his head lowered for several moments until the sensation at last began to pass.

The thought of illness rose up before him but he shook his head, dismissing it. He had never been ill, never suffered more than childish ailments or an occasional head cold; he wouldn't countenance the possibility of serious illness now.

The recollection flashed up in his brain that tomorrow was the day of Ted Gilchrist's funeral. He sighed deeply and passed a hand across his face. He had been grieved and shocked by the appalling accident.

Matt Shardlow, Ted's number two, was still on holiday and the accounts office was currently being run by the next man down, a bright, industrious young man who was coping well. Robert intended to promote Shardlow to chief accountant on his return from Majorca, move everyone else up a notch and advertise the resulting vacancy.

It should all work out very satisfactorily. Shardlow was able, with a forceful personality. He had been with the firm five years and was now forty-two, a very suitable age for the post.

The funeral was at three in the afternoon; Robert would head the contingent from the works. Ian Bryant had made himself very useful in helping to deal with the many details that had to be attended to after the tragedy. I'll miss Ian when he leaves, he thought, not for the first time. In another two weeks Ian would be off to another job; it had been arranged back at the start of the summer, before Ian came to Paragon.

It was purely by chance that their paths had crossed. One day at the beginning of June Robert had been driving back to the works after a business lunch, in haste to keep an appointment. There were roadworks ahead and he turned off to take a route along a succession of quiet side roads. He wasn't feeling well that day. Looking back on it, he realized that it was the beginning of the malaise he had later come to know better.

A couple of carloads of lads on their way to the races had caught up with him, had for some unknown reason taken an instant dislike to him or his vehicle, had decided to play games, boxing him in, nudging and bumping. He had felt too unwell to be able to deal with it and had pulled in to the side of the road. But his tormentors also pulled in, fore and aft. As they opened their doors and piled out, another car came up behind. The driver at once sized up the situation. He halted and got out, his manner easy and relaxed. He was a young man, casually dressed; his appearance didn't evoke the push-button hostility that Robert's had apparently done. In a very short time he had defused the situation and sent the lads on their way in good humour, with a couple of tips for the races.

Robert was anxious to reward the young man – Ian Bryant – in some way. Maybe he was in need of a job? He inquired about his circumstances and was told that Ian had worked until very recently as an administrative assistant for a manufacturing firm that was part of a large conglomerate. There had been a comprehensive reorganization during which Ian's job had vanished; he had been given generous redundancy pay. Shortly afterwards he was offered a job in an associate firm, in Martleigh, a town some twenty miles from Cannonbridge. It was a good position, similar to his previous job but with greater responsibility and better pay; the post was arising as a consequence of envisaged expansion. There was only one snag: the job wasn't due to start until mid-October. But that hadn't worried Ian, he had his redundancy money; he happily accepted the offer. He would, in the circumstances, be glad of work to occupy the next few months. And so it was arranged.

The unpleasant symptoms had now subsided but Robert's mind was at last made up: he would definitely make an appointment to see Dr Thornley. But he would say nothing about it to Lilian; no point in worrying her. He got to his feet and set off again along the paths. Time for another stroll before the Farrells arrived.

The Farrells were not, as Mrs Whiting believed, relatives of Robert's. Bridget Farrell was a first cousin, once removed, of Robert's first wife, Joan. Bridget had been a child of three when Robert and Joan married, a schoolgirl of thirteen when Joan died. Joan had always been fond of her and Bridget had often been over to Kincraig. Bridget had always been very friendly towards Robert but he could never rid himself of the feeling that there was something devious and underhand about her, even as a small child. He didn't believe she was all that genuinely fond of her Aunt Joan – as she called her – but manipulated her to get what she could out of her. Joan was always open-handed to Bridget in the way of gifts at birthday and Christmas, and many a time in between; she had also left Bridget a generous legacy.

Robert had seen a good deal less of Bridget after Joan's death but Bridget was punctilious about visiting him four or five times a year, the approaches on these occasions invariably coming from Bridget. She had taken a secretarial course after leaving school and had found a job in a solicitor's office in Wychford, where she still worked. She had grown up into a young woman with nothing much in the way of looks. Her nature seemed to Robert to have got progressively harder as the years went by but he kept on good terms with her, knowing that was what Joan would have wished.

Ten years ago Robert judged that the time had come to make a new will. He no longer had any living relatives, the last of them having died a few months earlier. He was certain that he would never remarry. Apart from minor legacies and charitable bequests he decided after a good deal of thought to leave everything to Bridget. He would never have particularly singled her out to take over the running of Paragon Tools after his death but the firm had to go to someone and Bridget could be considered a reasonably suitable candidate. She was sharply intelligent and must have acquired some knowledge of the world from her years in a solicitor's office. She had no romantic attachment that he knew of and certainly didn't appear, like some young women, to go in for a succession of fly-by-night boyfriends. And, most powerful argument of all, she was a relative of Joan's, Joan had loved her, and it had been Joan's money that allowed Paragon to take a great stride forward in its early days. Bridget surely had a strong claim in natural justice to be his heir.

He deemed it wisest not to tell Bridget she was to inherit the bulk of the estate. He would merely indicate to her casually in the course of conversation that she would not be forgotten in his will. When in due course he made this passing remark she received it in an equally nonchalant manner. Neither then nor at any subsequent time did she ever raise with him in even the most indirect fashion the question of what would happen to Paragon Tools after his death.

Four years ago he did remarry and another will must be drawn up. He now left the bulk of his estate to his new wife, being totally confident of her ability to run the firm and run it along lines he would approve of. Bridget's share of the inheritance would be limited to a sum of money substantial enough for Robert to feel he was treating her justly. All he said to Bridget about any of this was a word to the effect that his remarriage hadn't altered the fact that she would be remembered in his will. As before, she asked no questions.

Robert was all along aware, however much Bridget tried to hide it, that she was jealous of Lilian, resentful of her place in his life. He believed he could understand her feelings and never spoke of it to Bridget. Nor did he speak of it to Lilian – or she to him – although he knew she was too astute not to perceive it.

When the terms of the new will were being discussed, Cartwright, Robert's solicitor for thirty years, drew his attention to the possibility, by no means fanciful in this age of travel, that both he and Lilian might be involved in a road, sea or air accident in which both of them lost their lives or in which Robert lost his life but Lilian survived incapacitated, unable to run the business but with the likelihood of years of existence ahead of her. Robert thought it extremely unlikely that anything of the sort would ever happen but since the point had been raised he gave it his attention. He decided that if such a combination of circumstances should ever come about he would want a suitably funded trust set up to ensure that Lilian would be looked after in comfort for the rest of her life. The business and all remaining capital would go to Bridget. Again he made no mention of any of this to Bridget.

When Bridget married, a few months ago, Robert gave her a handsome cheque and wished her every happiness. He hadn't been particularly taken with her bridegroom, though he supposed Farrell was well enough in his way, and Bridget was plainly smitten with him.

At thirty-eight Keith Farrell was five years older than Bridget. Not bad-looking, Robert conceded, though he carried rather too much weight and had a self-indulgent look. And he was a touch too smooth-talking for Robert's liking. Farrell did seem to wish to inflate his own status, always referring to himself as an estate agent, though a question or two from Robert had speedily established that he wasn't even the manager of an estate agent's office but merely a member of the sales team. If by the age of thirty-eight Farrell hadn't risen to a managerial position, he would scarcely appear to be overendowed with business acumen and drive, nor did he strike Robert as a particularly hardworking type.

When Bridget had phoned to propose a visit this Sunday afternoon from herself and Keith, she had indicated that she wanted to ask Robert's advice. He had a shrewd notion that that meant she intended asking him for money. And he had an even shrewder notion that the initiative could have come from her husband.

He looked at his watch. Another brief stroll and then he would go in to his study, occupy the time till the Farrells arrived by looking through business papers and publications.

5

Ten miles away, in their trim semi on a newish estate on the outskirts of Wychford, the Farrells were preparing for their visit to Kincraig. Bridget had provided herself, as on every visit to Kincraig since Robert's remarriage, with a little gift of expensive confectionery for Lilian, in the mistaken belief that Lilian had a fondness for such items, a belief stemming from the warm thanks and manifest pleasure with which Lilian had greeted her first offering: a casket of handmade Belgian chocolates. Lilian had been anxious to foster good relations with Bridget and she was far too polite to reveal then or later that she didn't in fact have a sweet tooth; she continued to accept the presents with the same convincing show of lively appreciation. Bridget selected a different item for each visit; today it was a prettily ribboned box of sugared almonds.

Robert would have been surprised and disconcerted to learn

that Bridget was familiar with all the terms of his current will, as she had been with those of his previous will. Bridget had long been acquainted through her work with a woman by the name of Sylvie Murchison, a middle-aged spinster employed for many years as personal secretary to Cartwright, Robert's solicitor. Some years ago, Miss Murchison, who was devoted to her work, priding herself on meticulous and unremitting accuracy, had been guilty of a serious oversight in the course of a property transaction taking place between clients of the two firms of solicitors. Bridget had spotted the error in time and had drawn it most discreetly to Miss Murchison's attention before any damage was done. In the years that followed, Bridget had from time to time raised a query about Mr Anstey's current will, being always anxious in particular to know if any changes were being contemplated. Miss Murchison had managed to persuade herself that answering these queries was no more than a fair return for the service Bridget had rendered her.

Robert Anstey had guessed correctly that the purpose of the Farrells' visit today was to approach him for money. At her husband's urgent prompting Bridget intended asking Uncle Robert, as she called him, if he would consider advancing her now some or all of the money he was leaving her in his will. Keith had drawn her attention to an outstanding investment opportunity in the housing market, an opportunity that wouldn't last much longer. A backlog of dwellings, many of them repossessed by banks and building societies, still remained unsold after the collapse of the property market some time ago. The bulk of these properties had been well looked after by their owner-occupiers and were in sound order. Mass auction sales of this class of dwelling took place regularly, the buyers being in the main professional dealers, the prices achieved being markedly below normal values.

At the same time there existed in many areas an unsatisfied demand for properties to rent, would-be tenants being willing to pay very satisfactory rents. With his knowledge of the market and a decent amount of capital at his command, Keith was certain he could marry these two spheres of opportunity, buying cheap and renting out on shorthold leases for a very attractive return. In due course, when the market had fully recovered, the properties could be profitably sold or retained for rental, according to conditions at the time. He had all the facts and figures ready to expound.

6

Lilian Anstey had appropriated a back bedroom on the first floor at Kincraig for use as a combined study and office. She had an office of her own at Paragon Tools but she used it solely for her work for the firm. Her private correspondence, her studies and charity work were all dealt with at Kincraig.

She was hard at work this afternoon on her foreign language studies, making use of the interval before the Farrells were due to arrive. She had always had a flair for languages, achieving first-class grades at school and secretarial college. She had realized early on that proficiency in this area would be an increasingly valuable business asset and had never ceased honing her skills; she had made excellent use of them in every post she had held. Paragon had carried on a thriving export trade for many years and fresh markets were constantly opening up. She always enjoyed adding a smattering of some new language to her stock in trade, going on later, where practicable, to study it in greater depth.

The Farrells arrived prompt on time and were soon sitting down to tea, enjoying Mrs Whiting's delicious scones. The meal hadn't advanced very far before Robert made mention of what had brought the Farrells over today. 'I believe you wanted to ask my advice,' he said to Bridget with a neutral air, neither encouraging nor daunting.

She looked pleased at the invitation to unburden herself. 'We'd both be glad of your advice,' she replied with a fond glance at her husband, implying that in this respect, as in all others, they were of one mind. 'Your advice and your assistance,' she added with an appealing, girlish smile.

She leaned forward, fastening her gaze on Robert, speaking with great earnestness. 'You did say you would be leaving me some money in your will.' She clasped her hands and plunged into the spiel the two of them had so carefully prepared. Keith

28

sat by in supportive silence. The instant she finished speaking he reached for the briefcase he had set down by his chair and drew out a sheaf of papers and catalogues.

'If you'd care to look through these...' He passed them over to Robert. 'They'll put you in the picture.' Robert glanced through them. Lilian made no comment. She didn't ask to see any of the papers but sat with a look of mild interest on her face as if she were an outsider who had chanced to find herself present at some negotiation that had nothing to do with her.

Robert looked up from the papers to ask: 'What about your parents? Have either of you approached any of them for this money?'

Keith gave a wry smile. 'There wouldn't be a lot of point. None of them have anything to spare.'

'You've both worked ever since you left school,' Robert pointed out. 'How much have you saved between you?'

Keith gave another wry smile. 'Nothing, I'm afraid.'

'Do you have credit-card debts?'

He nodded.

'What do they amount to?'

'Maybe a thousand, fifteen hundred, between us.'

Robert regarded them both. 'You both run newish cars. You take foreign holidays. You lead active social lives, you visit theatres, cinemas, restaurants. If you want something, you buy it. If you haven't got the money, you buy it on credit.' He paused. 'I did without all those things when I was starting out. I started out from nothing. I saved every penny.' He spoke in clipped, unemotional tones. 'I didn't expect folk to hand me their hard-earned money on a plate, just for the asking. You don't get far in this life waiting to be spoonfed.' He gave Bridget a forthright look. 'My answer to your request is no. I'm not prepared to advance one penny of your legacy. I've no intention of subsidizing your husband in a property gamble.'

In the silence that followed, Bridget turned her head with slow deliberation and looked across at the large studio photograph of Joan Anstey in its silver frame, a photograph taken shortly after her marriage. She kept her gaze fixed on it for some moments before turning her head again and addressing Robert in a voice still easy and amicable but with a hint now of something less deferential simmering away underneath. 'I can't think that you got where you are today entirely on your own. You did have Aunt Joan's money to help you expand the business. And you did have this house and all its furnishings handed to you, as you would say, on a plate.'

Robert responded with a jerk of his head, his tone sharper now, his eye colder. 'I'd established Paragon Tools before I ever met Joan. She knew I was a responsible businessman. It was Joan who wanted to put her money into the business, I would never have asked her for it. If I'd died first, every penny I owned, the business and everything else, would have gone to Joan. She knew I would make proper use of the money, I wouldn't use it to gamble with.' He struck the table. 'That's all this housing venture is, an outright gamble. What you're proposing isn't honest manufacturing, it isn't sensible supply or service, all it is is an opportunity to profit from the misfortunes of others – if you're quick about it.' He flashed a look at Bridget. 'Joan would never have agreed to any of her money going into that kind of operation.'

Neither Bridget nor Keith made any further plea, any further attempt to argue their case. Lilian offered more tea, diplomatically opening up a fresh line of conversation. She soon had the visitors engaged in amiable chat. Robert remained silent for several moments, directing at each of the pair in turn a long assessing look before relaxing his features and joining easily in the talk.

7

For the first part of their drive home the Farrells didn't exchange a word, digesting all that had taken place during their visit, then Bridget erupted into speech. 'He had no right to refuse,' she declared with force. 'I have a moral claim to a good share of his money, however much he likes to hold forth about scrimping and saving, standing on one's own feet. And for all he makes out he was so fond of Aunt Joan, I don't for one single second believe he'd ever have dreamed of marrying her if she hadn't had the money and the house.' She fell silent again and then asked on a different note: 'Did you notice that look he gave me?'

'And me,' Keith rejoined. 'I could hardly help noticing.'

'What did you make of it? Do you think he might have thoughts of changing his will? Cutting down on what he's leaving me? Or cutting me out altogether?'

'It's possible,' Keith said slowly.

'I'll get on to Sylvie Murchison,' Bridget responded with energy. 'I'll ring her first thing in the morning. She'll let me know if he makes an appointment to see his solicitor.'

At seven o'clock Hester Whiting said good-night to the Ansteys before following her usual home-going practice of bolting the back door and checking that it was locked – she always entered and left by the side door. She would be back in Kincraig at nine in the morning, three-quarters of an hour before Lilian set off for Paragon; Robert would by then have been at his desk for an hour and a half.

As she took down her jacket from its peg she caught sight of her reflection in a nearby mirror. She paused for a moment to stare at her face, sighing briefly at her lack of looks. She put up a hand to tidy her hair, then sighed again and dropped her hand, assailed by a sudden wave of depression. What did it matter how she looked? There was no one to care.

Before her stretched another empty evening, the loneliness assuaged only by TV faces and voices, library romances. She put on her jacket, let herself out and set off for home.

In his ground-floor study Robert sat with his elbows on the table in the centre of the room, his chin propped on his hands. He stared fixedly ahead, reflecting on the Farrells' visit.

After some minutes he pushed back his chair and went over to the desk standing against the wall. He took out the copy of his will and returned to his seat. He glanced rapidly through the pages and then read certain paragraphs again, more slowly. He sat frowning, chewing his lip. Things had changed since the will was drawn up. Bridget was married now, Keith was very definitely someone to be taken into account. Two matters now must be reconsidered: Bridget's legacy and the future of Paragon if Lilian should be unable to take over after his death.

31

Various ideas floated up into his mind; two or three seemed worthy of further consideration. He made notes as he pondered.

Better have a word with his solicitor, he decided at last; see if Cartwright could come up with any useful suggestions. And he'd discuss it with Lilian over supper. Her views were always well worth hearing.

Supper was always later on a Sunday. Robert began to talk over his thoughts about the will as soon as he and Lilian sat down. He handed over his copy of the will for her to glance through and refresh her memory; she had been made aware of its contents when the will was drawn up.

She didn't give her views at once. She had no wish to interfere in what she saw as a family affair but if Robert wanted her opinion she would do her best to think up some arrangement which would be satisfactory all round, though she couldn't look on it as a very pressing problem. She could see no reason why Robert shouldn't live another twenty or twenty-five years and surely by that time the Farrells' marriage would either have strengthened into a lasting, trustworthy bond or would have long ago ended in divorce.

'If you try to attach conditions to the legacy,' she said, 'to stop Keith wheedling the money out of Bridget, I can't see how that could be done. Anything likely to be totally effective would be too restrictive to stand up in a court of law. Bridget could easily get it overturned. I should think the best you could do would be to divide her legacy into instalments to be paid out over, say, ten or fifteen years.' Robert inclined his head but made no comment.

'The other question, Bridget taking over if I was incapacitated,' she went on, 'I can't see how you could stop her, if she's really determined, giving control of the firm to Keith or, at the very least, making a good place for him in it, equal partner with herself, maybe. And I can't see how you could stop her handing over some or all of the other assets for Keith to use in some scheme of his own.' She smiled slightly. 'I think you're going to have to accept the fact that things would have to take their chance. Bridget will grow older and possibly wiser. She may not always be as smitten with Keith as she is now. She's clever enough, she might make a very good fist of things at Paragon.

32

And who knows? Keith might turn out to be a first-class businessman.'

She handed him back the copy of the will. 'I should certainly see Cartwright. He may know of some legal stratagem we're not aware of, though I wouldn't set your hopes too high on that.' She smiled again. 'In any case, I don't think you need lose any sleep over it. You're not going to die for a good many years and I've no intention of ending up a living vegetable after some dreadful accident.'

Robert rang the surgery as soon as it opened next day and was able to arrange to see Dr Thornley later in the morning. At nine o'clock he phoned his solicitor's office but was told Cartwright was not available; he had left on Saturday for four weeks' holiday in the Bahamas. He was offered an appointment with one of the other partners but declined it; he preferred to wait for Cartwright's return. He would ring again in, say, five weeks' time.

His visit to the surgery didn't prove very illuminating. Dr Thornley, a quiet, cautious man, duly questioned and examined him but expressed no opinion. 'I'd like you to see a consultant,' he told Robert. 'I should be able to get you an appointment in a week or so.'

Robert felt no anxiety but rather a measure of relief as he set off back to Paragon. At least he'd taken the first step.

Immediately on his arrival at work on Tuesday morning, the young man temporarily in charge of the accounts office went along to ask Robert's secretary if he might speak to Mr Anstey. Yes, it was important. He was admitted without delay.

He launched at once into a recital of various discrepancies that had come to light in the last week. His suspicions had been aroused within two or three days of taking over and by last Friday he had been pretty sure of his ground. He had decided to say nothing until this morning as he had thought it more seemly to wait until after Gilchrist's funeral and he couldn't see that an extra day or two would be of great significance. He had spent most of yesterday making one hundred per cent certain of the accuracy of his conclusions. He had delved further back in the books and had uncovered more discrepancies.

After hearing him out Robert rang a firm of auditors in a neighbouring town, a highly reputable concern specializing in fraud investigation; he had never previously had occasion to contact them. Shortly afterwards two men from the firm arrived to begin a survey of the books. Later in the morning the senior man informed Robert that they had seen enough to be certain fraud had been committed. He would leave his subordinate to continue the scrutiny. In the meantime he would advise inquiry into the personal and financial affairs of both Gilchrist and Shardlow. In such matters his firm regularly employed the discreet services of an agent whom he could thoroughly recommend.

At the end of Friday afternoon Robert came down the steps of the auditors' offices after a lengthy session and walked across to his car.

Detailed work was still going on but enough had now been done to form a reasonable hypothesis. The personal situations of Gilchrist and Shardlow had been looked into; they strongly suggested an ongoing need on the part of both men for an extra source of income. Gilchrist was supporting his mother-in-law in an upmarket residential home as well as financing his grandson's private education. Shardlow had had to meet the demands of a divorce settlement. It was abundantly plain that the operation of the fraud, which had been carried out with considerable skill, had required the involvement of both men.

The sums taken were never vast but there had been a steady drain over some years. The pair had started in a very small way and then, in the absence of repercussions, had grown bolder, gradually increasing the amounts before levelling off, their vital safeguard being the fact that they would never both be away from the office at any one time. Things might have continued indefinitely along these lines but for the chance of Gilchrist dying while Shardlow was on holiday.

Shardlow was due back at work on Monday and would probably return from Majorca on Saturday or Sunday. He would in all probability learn of Gilchrist's death before Monday morning and would have a very fair idea of the can of worms that had opened up in his absence. He could be expected to turn up at Paragon fully armoured, his defences ready. He was to be suspended on full pay as soon as he set foot inside the building.

Robert reached his car and got in. He hoped Lilian had no engagement for this evening; he very much wanted to talk over with her this matter of the fraud. The young man in Accounts, who now had a hopeful eye on promotion and was determined not to put a foot wrong, had scrupulously followed instructions and kept his lips tightly closed but Lilian, like everyone else at Paragon, could scarcely fail to be aware that an investigation was under way. Robert hadn't yet spoken of it to her, preferring to wait until he had solid fact to go on, and Lilian, as always, had asked no questions where plainly none would be welcomed. Now that he had today's report he felt discussing it with her would clarify his thoughts, help him to focus on what he now saw as the crucial point: what steps he should take after the inquiries were completed.

All at once he felt a surge of fatigue assail him. He leaned back against the upholstery and waited for it to pass. His appointment with the consultant had been fixed for next Monday afternoon. The consultant would undoubtedly pinpoint the source of the trouble, would prescribe some pills or course of treatment; he would feel better in no time at all.

The wave subsided. He sat up and switched on the engine. He drove out of the car-park, setting his face for home.

In reply to Robert's inquiry, made as soon as he walked in through the front door, Lilian told him her only engagement that evening was to sit with a twelve-year-old girl recently out of hospital after treatment for leukaemia; her mother wished to attend the meeting of her carers' group. Lilian had promised to be at the house by seven forty-five. 'I can't let her down,' she said. 'You don't have to,' Robert assured her. 'We can talk over supper.'

He lost no time in beginning as they sat down at the table. He outlined what had happened to date, together with the findings of the auditors and their inquiry agent. 'Their guess,' he told her,

35

'is that Shardlow was the initiator and persuaded Gilchrist to join him.' That squared with his own opinion of the two men. Gilchrist had been at Paragon for thirty years and Shardlow for only five; there was no indication of any fraud until four years ago. Shardlow was much the more dominant personality, altogether more foxy, with an agile brain; he would have had to involve Gilchrist in order to embark on the fraud at all.

Lilian listened with the keenest attention. Mrs Whiting, engaged in her usual duties of serving the meal, caught the drift of their conversation and grew intrigued. She could be very light of foot when it suited her, very unobtrusive, entering or leaving the dining-room.

'I can't see that the investigation can do anything but confirm Shardlow's guilt,' Robert said when he had covered the facts. 'It's what happens at that point that really concerns me.'

'Shardlow may see it as his best course to confess right away to some minor role in the fraud,' Lilian suggested. 'He might plead mitigating circumstances, explain his personal difficulties, put most of the blame – particularly the responsibility for initiating the fraud – on to Gilchrist. He might express deep contrition, beg forgiveness.'

Robert gave a short laugh. 'I can't see Shardlow begging for forgiveness.'

She smiled. 'No, I don't think I can, either.'

'And even if he did,' Robert added, 'it would make no difference to my attitude. It's easy enough to cry sorry when you've been found out.'

'Do the auditors suggest what you might do?' Lilian asked.

He moved his shoulders. 'They say it'll be up to me. They believe there's a fair chance a case could lie but there's also a chance Shardlow could wriggle free if he puts most of the blame on Gilchrist as the older man, the senior man, the prime mover.'

'A court case wouldn't come cheap,' Lilian pointed out.

'I realize that,' he acknowledged ruefully.

'And if the court didn't find the case proved or even found Shardlow not guilty, what then? He'd demand to return to work. Would you be prepared to reinstate him?'

He shook his head with vigour. 'I most certainly would not. I'm positive in my own mind he's guilty, whatever a court might find. I intend to be rid of him for good.'

'He might go to an industrial tribunal. You could lay yourself open to paying out substantial compensation for wrongful dismissal. It would be a good deal cheaper and quicker, a lot less hassle, to sidestep all that, court case and all. Just pay him to clear off for good.'

It would indeed, Robert reflected. Did he really want all that worry and vexation? He was no longer young, no longer so fit.

'In your shoes,' Lilian went on, 'I'd definitely take the easy way out. I'd cut my losses, buy him off. You could tell him you know exactly what the pair of them were up to, you're dispensing with his services, you'll never in any circumstances take him back or give him a reference. Provided he accepts all that and takes the money you offer in full discharge of any liability, you won't bring a court case. If he refuses, then he's welcome to go to a tribunal and you'll fight the case there, you'll call the auditors to give evidence.' She flung out a hand. 'I believe he'd see sense at that point even if he hadn't seen it before. I believe he'd take the money and be glad to get it, I believe you'd hear no more from him.'

'I see the force in everything you say,' Robert conceded. 'And I dare say it's what any solicitor would advise.' He shook his head slowly. 'But I can't think I could ever bring myself to do it.' He went on shaking his head. 'It would stick in my gullet.' He paused. 'I believe you've helped me to make up my mind. If the auditors' findings are what I'm sure they'll be, then I definitely will not let Shardlow off the hook. I'll bring a court case, whatever it costs. I couldn't let him get away with it and I certainly could never see myself handing over more of my hard-earned money to an employee I've trusted, a man who's been robbing me consistently for the last four years.'

8

Matthew Shardlow entered the Paragon building earlier than usual on Monday morning, but Robert and Ian Bryant were there before him. Robert had instructed Ian to await Shardlow's arrival in Accounts and convey him at once to Robert's office, making sure he had no opportunity to touch anything.

Robert said his piece to Shardlow, ending by informing him that he would be conducted from the premises forthwith and was under no circumstances to set foot in them again without authority.

Shardlow showed neither surprise nor any other emotion but listened throughout in silence, with a face of stone, stating in reply that he knew nothing of any misappropriation. He went on to say with an air of calm assurance that he would lose no time in seeing both his solicitor and his union representative. Before allowing himself to be escorted from the building he registered a formal protest at his treatment.

In the afternoon Robert had to spend more time than he had bargained for on his appointment with the consultant. He underwent a thorough examination, detailed questioning, a battery of tests. At the end of it all no diagnosis was pronounced, no opinion offered. He was given another appointment for Friday afternoon.

At around nine o'clock that same evening Matt Shardlow came out of his well-kept house on the Westway council estate. He had lived in the house since his marriage some sixteen years ago, seizing the chance to buy the property as soon as it became legally possible; he had been able to make the purchase without any need for a mortgage.

He was of average height, lean and sinewy. The light of the street lamps showed the face of a man who rarely smiled. Not exactly handsome but with his share of looks in a macho way. He had been an only child, born and brought up in a cottage not far from the council estate, the cottage where his widowed mother still lived. It had been Matt's home until he married; he still saw his mother most days.

His wife had left him seven years ago and he had lived alone since then. There were no children of the marriage and three years later there was a divorce by mutual consent. He had had to take out a mortgage to allow him to pay over to his wife the value of the half-share in the house she had been awarded under the settlement.

He left the estate and walked at a steady pace until he reached the neighbourhood where Robert Anstey lived. He hadn't gone haring off to consult either his solicitor or his union representative after being ushered out of Paragon; he hadn't in fact uttered one word of what had transpired there to a living soul.

He came within sight of Kincraig. There was no one about. He walked up and down without haste on the opposite side of the road, gazing fixedly across at the property, then he crossed over and went slowly up the drive, moving with silent agility, pausing every few yards to glance about and listen. In this fashion he arrived at the house.

The curtains were closed; light showed in a downstairs room. He surveyed the front and then began a leisurely circuit, ready at any moment to dart off into the shadows. Lights showed in other rooms; he could hear the sound of a TV or radio.

When he had completed the circuit to his satisfaction he stood staring at the house for several moments, his expression full of bitterness and resentment. Then he turned and went back down the drive with the same cat-footed tread.

Early on Friday afternoon Lilian Anstey returned to Paragon for an extra stint at Robert's request, as he had one or two outside appointments. Shortly before Robert was due to leave, Ian Bryant came along to his office to say a formal goodbye. Ian would be working as usual until five but he knew Robert wouldn't be coming back into the building again today and he wanted to express his appreciation of the kindness shown to him, the training he had received. He was due to start his new job in Martleigh on Monday morning.

He shook hands with Robert and Lilian, saying how much he had enjoyed working at Paragon. 'We're very sorry to lose you,' Robert told him. 'You know we'd have found you a good niche if you weren't contracted elsewhere.' The three of them came out of the office and stood in the doorway. 'If ever you do feel you'd like to come back,' Robert added, 'get in touch. I'm sure we could find you something you'd like.'

The door of a neighbouring office opened and Delphine Tate

came out. She stood for a moment regarding the group in the doorway before going off along the corridor.

On his way home after seeing the consultant Robert pulled into the first lay-by. He had insisted on the truth and he had been given the truth. He had believed himself prepared for anything and had at first been upheld by a kind of bravado. But that had by now worn off and he could no longer pretend that he was anything but totally devastated by what he had been told.

He would have to break the news to Lilian and he must do it without delay; the longer he put it off the harder he would find it. And delay would do Lilian no favours.

He was, it appeared, suffering from a comparatively rare disease of the central nervous system, progressive and ultimately fatal; the consultant had written down for him its long Latin name. The cause was at present unknown; there was possibly some genetic element. Research had been going forward for a number of years and would continue. So far it had produced little in the way of positive results.

There were medicines to alleviate the symptoms and always the hope of better medicines. He would need to cut down on his hours of work. He must get a certain amount of fresh air and exercise. His diet must be nutritious and easily digested; there should be as little stress and excitement as possible. It was of the utmost importance to ensure sufficient sleep, so if he intended to continue rising early, getting to work early, then he must get to bed early at night, eight thirty or nine, with only a small, light supper around six.

Above all he must strive to keep an optimistic outlook. There had been cases where patients no younger than himself had lived twenty years – though with what inexorably diminishing quality of life the consultant hadn't seen fit to spell out.

Robert sat staring out through the windscreen. He could have been carrying this time bomb about with him in happy ignorance all his life. Would the disease have affected his father in due course if that cliff-edge in Dorset hadn't crumbled under his feet? Or could his mother have bequeathed him this inheritance? She had died at the age of sixty, two years younger than he was

40

now. Maybe she had just escaped his fate – two years ago he had experienced none of his symptoms.

He leaned back in his seat. For the greater part of his existence he had never really believed that he would die one day; it had seemed an impossible notion. He had always known in his head that death was the inescapable fate of all living creatures but knowing it in the head was a far cry from knowing it in the guts.

He closed his eyes. His mother had turned to religion when her health began to fail. And Joan, his first wife, had always been a deeply religious woman; she had drawn great comfort from her beliefs in the last weeks of her life. Neither he nor Lilian had ever been religiously inclined, though they both attended church as social occasion demanded. Neither could look now to religion for any solace.

Another car drove into the lay-by, breaking in on his thoughts. He sat up and looked at his watch. He must be getting home; Lilian would be wondering where he was. If she had no engagement this evening he would put off breaking the news until supper was over and Mrs Whiting had gone home. He must put as brave a face on it as possible. He switched on his engine and pulled out.

A church clock was striking seven when Matt Shardlow turned into the road leading to Kincraig. As he approached the property on the other side of the road he saw a woman come out of the driveway and walk in his direction. He drew back into the shadows. The woman walked at a good pace, looking down, sunk in thought; she didn't see him.

He stared across at her with a critical gaze. Her figure appeared reasonably slim. He got a look at her face under a street lamp; it seemed passable.

She turned the corner and was lost to sight. He set off again towards Kincraig, walking slowly now, pondering.

Yes, she could be considered a possibility. Just about.

Lilian had no engagement for Friday evening. After the meal, when they were settled in the sitting-room, she said gently:

'You've been very quiet this evening. You ate hardly anything. Are you still worrying about the fraud investigation?'

'No, it isn't that.' Robert paused. 'I saw a consultant today.' He told her in a calm, controlled manner everything he had been told himself. She had a right to know; in her shoes he would want the whole truth.

She didn't speak until he had finished. He saw, in spite of her strong effort to conceal it, that it had come as a tremendous shock. But she was as positive in her response, as kind and supportive as he had known she would be. She got up from her chair, went over and gave him an affectionate kiss, knelt down beside him and laid a hand on his. 'You know I'll do anything I can to help.' Her voice shook. 'In any way at all.'

The phone rang in the hall and she stood up to answer it. It was Bridget Farrell. 'I'm glad I've caught you,' Bridget said. 'I wanted to ask if it would be all right if Keith and I came over to tea on Sunday. We both felt our last visit didn't go as well as it might, we felt we rather upset Uncle Robert.' She hesitated. 'I wouldn't want him to get the wrong impression about Keith, to think badly of him.' She added in a rush: 'Don't worry, it isn't about money. We don't want to ask him for anything at all, we'd just like to get things back on a good footing again.'

Lilian was still in a state of shock; she had had not the slightest inkling that anything was wrong with Robert's health. She strove now to keep the tremor from her tone. 'I quite understand,' she told Bridget. 'I'm sure it's a good idea but this Sunday may not be the best time to come over.'

Bridget's sharp ears had caught the unsteady note in her voice. 'Is anything wrong?' she asked.

Lilian didn't answer that but said: 'Would you mind holding on for a moment? I'll just have a word with Robert.'

She returned to the sitting-room and told Robert of Bridget's request. 'Would you like to see them?' she asked. 'Or shall I put them off?'

He grimaced. 'I'm not in the mood for the pair of them at the moment. Tell them to leave it for the present.' He smiled. 'But put it civilly.' She was about to leave the room again when he added: 'I think you'd better tell Bridget about the illness. She'll have to know sooner or later. It might as well be now, we've no reason to keep it from her.'

'Would you rather speak to her yourself?' Lilian asked.

Again he grimaced. 'No, I would not. I'll leave it to you – if you don't mind.'

'No, of course not,' she responded warmly.

She went back to the phone and gave Bridget the information in as matter-of-fact a fashion as she could manage. Bridget was taken aback; she had seen no signs of anything amiss. She was voluble in her expressions of astonishment, distress, sympathy, readiness to help.

'I'll pass on your messages,' Lilian told her. 'And I'll be sure to let you know if there's any way either of you can help.' It might be best, she went on to say, not to make a formal visit next time but just to look in casually and briefly, on the off-chance, if they happened to be over this way.

Bridget was up early next morning. She was on the doorstep of the public library when it opened at nine thirty. By nine forty she was installed at a table in the reference room, earnestly perusing a selection of medical tomes, pausing from time to time to make a careful note.

9

Monday morning was bright and crisp, with a chill breeze. A minute or two after one o'clock Matt Shardlow, smartly dressed and groomed, set his finger on the Kincraig doorbell. His ring was answered by Hester Whiting. Matt asked if he might speak to Mr Anstey.

'He's not here,' Hester told him. 'He's not coming home for lunch today.'

'I happened to be passing,' Matt explained, 'and it struck me he might be here. I thought I'd take a chance and try to see him. I know he comes home to lunch sometimes.'

'Yes, he does,' she confirmed, 'but not very often. They're neither of them here today. Is it a business matter?'

'Yes, it's to do with Paragon,' he told her. 'I've worked there for five years but I'm laid off at present – because of a misunderstanding. I thought if I could get a word in private with Mr Anstey, man to man, away from the works, I could get it sorted.'

A quality of sharp attention entered her gaze. 'May I ask your name?' she inquired.

'Shardlow,' he answered. 'Matthew Shardlow.' He grinned. 'Generally known as Matt.'

'Shardlow,' she repeated, looking at him with increasing interest.

'Are you the housekeeper here?' he asked in a friendly manner.

She nodded.

'Have you worked here long?'

'No, not long.' There was a brief pause. She gave a little shiver. 'It's chilly today. I was going to make myself some coffee before I go off. I don't know if you'd like a cup?'

'I would indeed,' he answered heartily. 'It's kind of you to offer.'

She stepped back and held the door wide. 'You'd better come in then.'

The Westway council estate had a superior end and a somewhat rougher end, with the greater part of the estate lying in between. Matt Shardlow's house was situated in this intermediate region.

His father, a small-time general dealer, had always had an interest in old furniture and had set up a workshop in the cellar of his cottage where he repaired and restored such pieces as came his way and appeared to warrant the treatment. Matt had begun helping him as soon as he was old enough to pass his father the right tool. When Matt was seventeen his father died. Matt had just left school and begun work in the office of an auction saleroom.

During the time he worked there he was able to put in bids for dilapidated items of furniture as well as for the boxes of unlisted oddments from house clearances that went for very little. These boxes always appealed to Matt, offering as they did the perpetual hope of coming across some real find among the tat.

When he left the saleroom office after a year or two, in search of greener pastures, he kept his link with the auction rooms and had never ceased his small-scale buying and selling, restoring and dealing. He had retained his father's workshop, still keeping it on after his marriage – there was no room in his council house for a decent workshop.

Shortly after six on Monday evening Matt opened his front door a little way and glanced about. No one in sight. 'Get on then,' he commanded the lad standing behind him. 'Don't hang about.'

The lad thrust out his lips in a mutinous line. 'You should have given me more than that.' He flung out a hand, opened his fingers, stared down at the coins on his palm. 'It was worth more than that.'

Matt half swung round with a threatening gesture. 'Clear off! Think yourself lucky I take your stuff at all.'

The lad, Billy Coleman by name, backed down at once. He had experience of Matt's uncertain temper.

'And put that money away in your pocket,' Matt instructed. Billy did so and Matt opened the door a little wider, glancing out again. Still no one about. 'Go on, get off home,' he ordered. Billy darted swiftly out and Matt instantly closed the door behind him.

Billy lived at the rougher end of the estate. The moment he rounded the first corner he stopped to pull out the handful of coins, check the amount rapidly again. He dropped the coins back in his pocket and set off at speed for home. He was ten years old, small and slight for his age, with cropped fair hair, an alert look. As soon as he got home the money would go into the box hidden under his bed. It was safe there; any cleaning of his room was done entirely by himself.

As he ran he calculated the total amount he would now have. It was steadily increasing but still far from enough. It was his runaway fund, the money he would need when he set off in search of his father. It was hard to judge exactly how much more he would have to come by but instinct told him it was better to set the figure too high rather than too low. The last thing he would want would be to start out full of hope, run out of funds before he found his Dad and be forced to return home with his tail between his legs.

He turned the last corner and halted from force of habit. Home was the farther half of the first pair of semis and he had good reason to be wary of Ormerod, the solitary occupant of the nearer half. But there was no sign of Ormerod now. He went quickly by and in through his own gate.

His stepmother, Glenna, was upstairs in her bedroom when Billy let himself into the house. She was getting ready to go to work. She was a barmaid in a club and rarely reached home before two in the morning, rarely rose before eleven.

She called out to Billy and he went along to her bedroom doorway. Clothes were strewn over the bed, there was a strong smell of perfume. Glenna stood before the mirror, dolled up, ready for the evening, tweaking into place errant strands of her brightly blonded hair. She was thirty-eight years old, good-looking in a fashion that lacked all subtlety; she had been careful to keep her figure.

She picked up a can of hairspray and directed the jet at her locks with practised skill. She didn't glance at Billy. 'I'm off now,' she told him. 'I have to go in early, they're short-handed.' She usually left the house at seven fifteen. 'Don't make any noise in the morning.' She neither liked nor disliked Billy; he was merely a fact in her life. In precisely the same way Billy neither liked nor disliked her. He had learned early on that she had a temper which he took care not to provoke.

He turned without replying and went across the landing into his own room. It was tidy enough, clean enough. A pile of football magazines was neatly stacked on a shelf. He closed the door and stood motionless, listening until he heard Glenna go down the stairs and out of the house. He waited for the sound of her car driving off before he moved.

He took a few steps and reached down under the bed for his box. He took the coins from his pocket and added them to one of the plastic bags inside. He took an old envelope out of the box and drew from it a snapshot showing signs of much handling. It had been taken five years ago and showed his parents and himself walking along a seaside promenade. His mother had died a year later. He could still remember her. She had been quiet and gentle; he had loved her dearly. But her memory was growing steadily fainter; he could no longer recall the tone of her voice. Every day without fail he took out the snapshot, the only one he had, and studied it with deep concentration, striving to keep her alive in his mind.

After a minute or two he put the snapshot back in its envelope and returned the box to its hiding-place. He took off his jacket and went along to the bathroom to wash his hands before eating, as his mother had taught him long ago.

Downstairs in the kitchen there was the usual assortment of snacks to choose from; in the fridge a selection of the club left-overs Glenna regularly brought home. He put what he wanted on a plate and carried it into the living-room. He switched on the TV and sat down to eat and watch.

His father had married Glenna three years ago. At that time she was working in a pub; it was there that the two had met. Coleman was a scaffolder by trade, accustomed when his first wife was alive to earning good money, able to move around the county with the gang, wherever work took them. After his wife's death he could take only local work as there was no one he could ask to look after Billy. In consequence he found himself earning a good deal less. And he missed the itinerant life, the matiness of the gang; he found it irksome to be confined to the same town, day in, day out.

He saw marriage to Glenna as the solution to his problems. Once the ring was on her finger he lost no time in going back to his old way of working. Glenna had no complaints; he brought home good wages and didn't keep her short. It had been a marriage of convenience on both sides though each had mistakenly believed the other to be motivated, at least in part, by genuine affection. Glenna had been living in a bedsit and had always had a longing for a house of her own. On the whole she had been satisfied with her bargain. She saw little of her husband and that suited her well enough. She had never had to bother with cooking or housework and she didn't bother with them after her marriage. Billy she found scarcely any trouble; she had let him see from the start that she was someone to be reckoned with. He looked after himself, got himself off to school in the mornings, never got into trouble, never cheeked her, never complained.

But if Glenna had no complaints, Coleman was far from satisfied with his side of the bargain. Glenna had shown a very different side of herself once they were married. He had taken it for granted that she would look after Billy properly, would cook, see to the laundry and generally run the household in as

47

caring and competent a fashion as his first wife had done. He had expected her to continue to be as good-tempered and welcoming as he had always found her before their marriage. But on all these counts he very soon found himself sadly mistaken. He wasn't a man to make scenes; his nature was to withdraw inside himself when things went awry.

He endured it for eighteen months and then decided to endure it no longer. He knew where there was work going abroad with good pay and he took himself off without a word to either Glenna or Billy. Glenna received a letter from him soon afterwards, posted before he left England. It revealed neither his new address nor the name of his new employers. It merely informed her he wouldn't be coming back but would be sending money every month via a bank.

Glenna didn't mind; in fact it suited her very well. She left her job in the pub and got herself another with much better pay and many more pickings at the club.

When she passed on to Billy the news that his Dad wouldn't be back, Billy made no reply; he simply didn't believe it. Of course his Dad would be back, either to stay for good or to fetch him, take him off to live with him wherever it was he had landed up.

The days went by, turning into weeks and months. Glenna hardly ever gave a thought to her vanished husband. There was always someone to dance attendance on her from among the club regulars. She was better off, better settled, better suited all round than she'd ever been.

After twelve months or so the money stopped coming from Coleman. There was no word in explanation and the bank manager was no wiser than Glenna. She took it philosophically; it had always been on the cards. He would surely by now have met someone else, maybe even got his new ladylove pregnant. These things happened and as far as she could see there was nothing she could do about it.

Her husband's name was still on the council rent book but that was no drawback as long as she kept paying the rent, which she had every intention of doing. Keeping a roof of her own over her head was extremely important to her.

More than one of her men friends was willing to embark on a more settled relationship. She knew that would be the smart thing to do, as long as she picked the right man. But she could see no immediate reason for hurry. She was well enough as she was, playing the field, keeping her freedom – but only for as long as she kept her looks. As soon as they began to go her earnings would take a tumble; she would be downgraded first to waitressing, then to cloakroom work, ending, as like as not, as a cleaner. She was determined none of that would happen to her. She could rely on her mirror to tell her when the moment had come to say goodbye to liberty a second time and settle for security. That day, she acknowledged frankly to herself, could not be indefinitely delayed. But she couldn't grumble; she'd had a good run for her money.

On this Monday evening Billy sat watching the TV programmes with varying attention. Just before seven there came a ring at the front door. He opened it to find one of his stepmother's men friends, Tom Palmer, standing before him. Palmer had started coming to the house not long after Glenna began working at the club but she had dropped him a few months back.

He was in his early forties, tall and quite good-looking. He was a widower with a grown-up son; he owned the flat in which he now lived alone. He was inclined to drink too much on occasion and was given in drink to jealous outbursts which could sometimes lead to violence. This was why Glenna had parted company with him; one thing she would never take from a man was being used as a punchball.

From time to time Palmer would appear on the doorstep to try to make it up with Glenna, who always gave him short shrift. There had never been any love lost between Palmer and Billy.

Palmer demanded now to speak to Glenna. It was plain that he had been drinking. 'She's not here,' Billy told him, civilly enough. 'She's gone to the club.'

'Don't give me that,' Palmer retorted. 'She never goes this early.'

'She had to go in early this evening.' Billy began to slide the door gently forward. 'They're short-handed.'

'You're lying!' Palmer made an ineffectual lunge at him. 'I know she's in there. I've got to talk to her.'

Billy swung the door shut in his face, releasing the catch on the lock. Palmer hammered on the panel, demanding to be let in.

Billy ran through to the back door to make sure it was locked and bolted, then he ran upstairs to the landing window overlooking the front garden. After a minute or two the hammering and calling ceased and Palmer went off down the path and out through the gate. He got into his car and drove away.

Billy went back to his TV, being careful to keep an eye on the time. When the clock showed eight thirty he stood up and went round the house, checking that everywhere was secure, drawing all the curtains. He left a light on in his bedroom and his radio playing. He put on his jacket, slipping his torch into a pocket. Downstairs in the living-room he left on a light and the TV.

He eased open the front door and peered out into the autumn evening. No one in view. He took a few steps outside, giving particular attention to the adjoining semi. No sign of Ormerod, though a light showed downstairs.

Ormerod was a bachelor, a strongly built man in his sixties; he worked as a van driver for a scrap-metal merchant with premises on the outskirts of Cannonbridge. He owned his semi; he had shared it with his mother until her death a few years back. He had never been a mixer and had grown steadily more morose since she died. Some time later he acquired a dog of dubious ancestry as a companion for himself and to guard the house. When he was out, the dog was kept on a long chain at the side of the house, allowing it to patrol front and back.

The local children in this rougher end of the estate soon developed a taste for baiting the animal until it strained on its chain, leaping into the air, trying in vain to get at them. Billy's father went next door on more than one occasion to complain to Ormerod about the nuisance from the barking but he got little joy.

Then came a spell of national hysteria about pit bull terriers. Every tabloid newspaper carried its story of savage beasts attacking, terrifying, mauling. Somewhere in the ancestry of Ormerod's animal there might conceivably have been some minute strain of the pit bull terrier though it would have needed the eye of faith to detect it. One day while Ormerod was at work a gang of excited children stoned the creature to death.

Ormerod was devastated but he recognized that there was little he could do. He had no evidence as to the identity of the culprits and he knew he would get no help from local parents.

He didn't report the incident, believing, probably correctly, that he would receive little sympathy from the police. He had never kept a dog since.

Billy was a mere seven years old at the time. He had never joined in the tormenting and had had no hand in the dog's death. But Ormerod couldn't separate the complaints made by Coleman from the attack on the dog. He went next door to voice his loud and bitter anger; he wouldn't be persuaded by any protestations of innocence on Billy's part. Billy made sure forever after to keep out of his way, particularly after his father left home and he felt himself a good deal more vulnerable.

Now he took a few more cautious steps along the path. Still no sign of Ormerod. He turned and went noiselessly back to close the front door, then he made his way swiftly and silently down the path to the gate, ready to dart off like the wind if Ormerod should suddenly appear.

Shortly after nine Matt Shardlow drove along the quiet lane leading to his mother's cottage. He parked his vehicle, a large estate car a few years old, in the spot where he always left it, round the back, by the door giving access to the cellar workshop. There was a light on in the cottage and he could plainly hear the voice of the TV newscaster – his mother was hard of hearing and always had the sound well turned up.

He didn't immediately announce his presence, didn't let himself in through the front door with the key he had always kept but did what he often did: unlocked the cellar door and carried down the steps various items from the back of the car. He occupied himself in the cellar for some time before ascending the stairs into the house, going along to the living-room and beating an identifying tattoo on the door panel. His mother gave him a fond smile of welcome as he entered. She was seventy years old, a gentle, kindly woman, stout and slow of movement, troubled by arthritis.

She asked Matt to turn off the TV and he sat down close by her. They began an animated exchange of news and gossip, questions and answers about her state of health, things that needed doing in the house and garden, though his last visit had been as recently as the previous afternoon. She didn't ask how long he had been on the premises, she didn't ask if he had been into the workshop or what he did down there. She had never found asking questions of her son a fruitful exercise and had long ago abandoned it. She had very rarely set foot in the cellar when her husband was alive and had never once set foot in it since his death, nor had she the slightest wish to. Whatever her precious Matthew did or thought or wanted was perfectly all right by her. That wholly uncritical attitude had been her guideline in all her dealings with her husband; it was her guideline in her dealings with her son.

It had never crossed her mind, after Matt's wife left him, to suggest he should sell his house and move back in with her. She was sure he would marry again. And she continued to see plenty of him, as she had done throughout his marriage, so she had no complaints on that score.

He had felt constrained to tell her he had been suspended from Paragon as he knew the information wouldn't be long in reaching her from other sources. 'It's just a misunderstanding,' he assured her. 'Ted Gilchrist had got the books in a bit of a muddle. He was getting past it. I was forever spotting some mistake he'd made, having to put it right.'

She asked him now if he had heard anything from Paragon. He told her no, he wouldn't expect to hear just yet. He got to his feet and went off to make her usual hot drink. When he came back with it they chatted easily of other things. He kissed her an affectionate goodbye as he always did. He didn't say: 'See you tomorrow'; he never said that. She didn't ask when he would be looking in again; she never asked.

10

Neither Robert nor Lilian Anstey was home for lunch on Tuesday so Hester Whiting was able to leave Kincraig on the dot of one fifteen. She set off for home with a light in her eye, a spring in her step. For once she had something of real interest, not to say excitement, to attend to before returning to work at four thirty. Yesterday morning, when she was again alone in the house, Matt Shardlow had called for the third time. Over coffee and biscuits in the kitchen he had asked her out and she had instantly accepted. They were to run out tomorrow evening to a quiet country hotel for dinner; he would pick her up at home at seven fifteen. When she had first started work at Kincraig Mrs Anstey had told her that if she ever wished to leave earlier than seven on any particular evening she had only to say so. Now for the first time she would be making use of that permission, though she judged it wisest not to tell Mrs Anstey exactly why.

There was much to be done before tomorrow evening. She had already spent time yesterday giving an extra clean and polish to her house; she had made some particularly pleasing arrangements of flowers from her garden. She had fixed an appointment to have her hair done tomorrow afternoon – a greatly daring step, as she had never in her life so much as crossed the threshold of a salon.

A serious bout of shopping was the plan for this afternoon; she had to provide herself with a whole new outfit. A dress and jacket, a pair of shoes, light and elegant, a little handbag to match. She had bought nothing new in a very long time and she had never bought anything in the slightest degree frivolous. It had always been the most serviceable garments at the keenest prices. She was seized now with a spirit close to recklessness; she could well afford to splurge.

She reached home in record time and let herself in. She cast an eye over the living-room to see how it would strike a first-time visitor. Quite passable on the whole, she judged, but one small change she did make: she took the framed photograph of her late husband and with barely a glance at it put it away, face down, in a drawer.

When Delphine Tate left Paragon on Tuesday at the end of the day's work she didn't go straight home but set off for town to buy some groceries. She was on the point of entering a supermarket when she spotted Ian Bryant some yards away, walking in her direction. She halted and stood waiting for him. He slowed as he neared the supermarket and suddenly caught sight of her. She stepped forward, smiling. 'Hello, there,' she said lightly. 'I didn't expect to see you. Are you going inside?' She jerked her head at the supermarket entrance.

That was precisely what he had been about to do. He had come over to Cannonbridge in the course of his duties to attend a routine meeting at an associate firm. He had decided to call in at the supermarket for a few items before driving back to the flat he rented in Martleigh.

But he had no intention of getting ensnared by Delphine. He shook his head. 'No, I'm not. I'm on my way home.' He saw no reason to enlighten her about what he was doing in Cannonbridge.

She inquired about his job, if he liked it, how he was getting on. He answered pleasantly enough: he liked it very well, he believed he was doing all right.

She related bits of Paragon news and gossip. 'I'm doing more work for Mrs Anstey now,' she told him. 'She comes in more often these days. Mr Anstey's started taking more time off.' Without any pause she went on to ask him where he was living now.

He wasn't going to satisfy her curiosity. 'I'm comfortable enough,' he answered.

'Where exactly is it?' she pressed him.

But he wasn't to be badgered. 'In a nice enough district,' he replied amiably.

She saw she was getting nowhere with that line of approach and abandoned it for another tack, suggesting they might meet sometime when he had an evening free. He regretted that he was rather busy at present.

'Later, maybe?' she offered.

'Maybe.' His tone was non-committal.

As he went on his way she remained for a moment gazing after him. He didn't turn his head to look back at her.

She set her jaw. I'm not giving up on you yet, my lad, she said to herself as she went into the supermarket. She wasn't admitting defeat that easily.

At five minutes past two on Wednesday afternoon Hester Whiting arrived at the hairdressing salon for her two fifteen appointment. As she took a seat to await her call she noticed a display of

54

perfume and cosmetics in a side area through an archway. She made her mind up on the instant. After she'd had her hair done she would go in there and ask for advice about a little light make-up; she had never used cosmetics of any kind. And perfume – she'd ask to try two or three before making up her mind. A feeling of joyous adventure rose inside her. She felt able at last to give way to impulses suppressed for so many years.

When the hairdresser sat her down before the mirror a few minutes later he took her measure in a single all-embracing glance. She wouldn't look at all bad, he thought as he studied her reflection, if she presented herself better. He asked what she had in mind.

She would like her hair nicely styled, she told him, washed and set. She experienced another sudden leap of courage, perceiving all at once that there was no virtue in remaining mousy all her life. 'And I'd like it tinted,' she added boldly. Nothing extreme or unsuitable, she went on to explain, no trying too hard to look young, just something to brighten up her appearance.

He loosened her hair, let it fall about her shoulders, began to comb it through. Plenty of it, in good condition; never been permed, bleached or dyed. A promising start, at all events. He saw that her eyes were an intriguing shade of amber. He could use a tint that would set them off.

He picked up his scissors, made one or two preliminary snipping passes in the air, smiled at her face in the glass.

'Right, then,' he said with relish. 'Let's get cracking.'

11

Lew Dutton, Glenna Coleman's currently most favoured man friend, called in to see her early on Wednesday evening. He was forty-five years old, unremarkable in looks and build; he was a supervisor in the packing department of a Cannonbridge mail order firm. The pair of them sat in the kitchen, conversing in low tones while Billy watched TV in the living-room, alert all the while for any development in the kitchen that might concern himself. He was no fonder of Dutton than of any of Glenna's other men, disliking them all on principle as potential usurpers of his father's place.

After he had been watching TV for some fifteen minutes he heard the two of them emerge from the kitchen. They came along to the living-room. Glenna gestured to Dutton to take his seat on the sofa, then she went over and switched off the TV. Billy braced himself against whatever might be coming. Glenna plonked herself down beside Dutton. Billy continued to stare at the blank screen.

Dutton addressed Billy in a wheedling tone. 'I've got a couple of new videos.' He mentioned the titles. 'You can borrow one of them. Both of them, if you like. I could pop them over tomorrow.'

Billy kept his gaze fixed on the screen. 'No, thanks,' he replied in a voice devoid of all expression. It was by no means the first time that Dutton had tried to win Billy over, offering to take him to a football match or the cinema. All his approaches had met with the same cool response.

'Don't be so bloody rude,' Glenna suddenly burst out at Billy. Dutton flashed her a warning glance but she ignored it. 'Lew's only trying to be friendly. Why can't you meet him half-way?' Billy remained silent.

'You'd better start making the effort,' she flashed out at him. Dutton laid a restraining hand on her arm but she shook it off. 'Lew's going to be moving in here.'

Billy was shaken out of his resolute control. 'He can't do that! You wouldn't dare! What would Dad say when he comes back?'

Glenna gave a short, snorting laugh. 'Your precious Dad's never coming back! You'd better get that into your head. He's gone for good.'

'He *is* coming back!' Billy cried. 'He *is*! He *is*! He'd never go away for ever!'

'That's just what he has done!' she flung back at him. 'We'll neither of us ever lay eyes on him again.' She gestured at Dutton. 'Here's Lew, ready to be friendly. You should think yourself lucky. A lot of men wouldn't stand for someone else's kid round the place. But Lew's willing to take you on, treat you right.'

'What do you say?' Dutton's tone was still wheedling. 'Can't we be mates?'

56

Billy sat in mutinous silence.

Glenna started in on him again. 'You'd better get it into your head – ' but Dutton broke in on her with a quick 'Leave it!'

'No! I won't leave it!' she retorted. 'He's got to be taught he can't go laying down the law about what I do or don't do, who comes here or doesn't come here. He should think himself lucky I keep him here at all. He's no kin of mine, I've got no responsibility for him.' She turned the full glare of her gaze on Billy. 'Lew's definitely going to move in here, whether you like it or not. You'd better make up your mind to show him some respect or you'll find yourself out on the street or in care. See how you like that.'

Billy sat as if he hadn't heard.

'We're off on Friday for a break,' Glenna went on, her tone marginally less strident. The local schools would be closing on Friday afternoon for a week's half-term holiday. 'Lew will be moving in here after we get back. You can think about it while we're away. Make up your mind to behave sensibly and we'll all get along all right.'

The weather continued calm and bright. Shortly after six on Friday evening Lew Dutton pulled up in front of the Colemans' house. Glenna was packed, ready to leave; they were going to a caravan on the south coast. Lew carried her cases out to the car and stowed them away in the boot.

In the kitchen Glenna was issuing final instructions to Billy. She didn't give him the address of the caravan and he didn't ask for it. 'We'll be back on the Sunday evening,' she told him. 'That's the 27th, nine days from now. I can't say what time we'll be back, it could be late. There's no telling what the traffic might be like.'

Dutton came into the kitchen as she was putting some money into a jar. 'That should be more than enough,' she said and reached down to put the jar away in a cupboard.

'Hang on!' Dutton took the jar from her and added another couple of notes before handing it back. 'Just in case,' he said to Billy with a cajoling smile. Billy didn't look at him, he made no acknowledgment but stood mute and motionless.

'That doesn't mean you can go blueing it all,' Glenna said as she put the jar away and closed the cupboard door. 'That extra's just for emergencies, if you're really stuck, though I can't see why you should be.' She'd been away twice before, with other men, leaving Billy on his own; there had been no mishaps. This would be her longest absence; her two previous jaunts had been for long weekends. She hadn't left her address with Billy on those previous occasions; it hadn't occurred to either of them that she should do so.

Billy didn't go out to the car with them to wave them off but their departure was observed by Ormerod next door. He was working on his van, on the area of hard-standing at the side of his dwelling.

Twenty minutes later Ormerod saw another car pull up outside the Colemans' house, a car that had often stopped there earlier in the year.

Tom Palmer got out of the car and let himself in through the Colemans' gate. He went across to the garage and looked in through the window, then he went up to the front door and rang the bell. When Billy answered his ring he asked in a peremptory fashion to speak to Glenna.

'She's not here,' Billy told him.

'You little liar!' Palmer threw at him with heat. 'I know she's in. Her car's in the garage.'

'She's not here,' Billy repeated. 'She's gone on holiday.'

'Who's she gone with?' Palmer demanded.

'Nothing to do with you who she's gone with,' Billy replied calmly.

'It's Lew Dutton, isn't it?'

'None of your business,' Billy maintained.

Palmer lunged at him and Billy made to slam the door against him. But he was too late. Palmer seized him by the shoulder and dragged him out on to the step, fetching him a sharp clout on the head with his other hand. Billy managed to wriggle free and darted off round the side of the house. Palmer was about to go after him when he became aware of Ormerod who had straightened up from his work on the van and stood watching him. After a moment Palmer swung round and went off down the path to his car. As he drove away Billy ran back inside the house and closed the door.

12

Robert Anstey had been feeling low for the past day or two and had been doing his best to disguise the fact. He made an effort at easy conversation as he and Lilian sat down to supper on Wednesday evening. Supper was earlier now, always a very light meal as far as Robert was concerned. He knew Lilian had a committee meeting for one of her charities at seven forty-five. After she had gone he would be able to sit back in his easy chair and do nothing at all, free of the need to make any kind of effort.

When Hester Whiting had brought in the dishes and left the room he observed with an attempt at lightness: 'Mrs Whiting's looking a lot smarter lately. She's changed her hairstyle and done something to the colour. I'd hardly take her for the same woman.' He smiled. 'Do you suppose she's found herself a boyfriend?'

Lilian moved her shoulders. She wasn't greatly interested in Mrs Whiting's appearance or her possible love life. 'I thought I'd look through my dresses before I go out,' she said. 'I'll try on one or two, see which you think would be best for Friday evening.' She was attending a dinner on Friday for another of her charities and it was important to look her best; she had a report to deliver in the form of a speech.

'Yes, of course I'll give my opinion,' Robert told her, 'though you'll look lovely, whatever you decide to wear. I'm only sorry I won't be coming with you.' She reached out and touched his hand, gave him a tender smile.

They didn't linger over the meal and as soon as it was finished she went up to her bedroom, across the landing from Robert's. She opened her wardrobe and ran her hand along the rail, assessing, considering. She made a selection and carried the dresses over to the bed, laying them carefully down. She held each in turn up against herself before the long mirror, set aside two and put the rest back in the wardrobe. She slipped out of her skirt and blouse and into the first dress. She went swiftly down to the sitting-room to execute a turn or two in front of Robert before hurrying back upstairs to repeat the performance with the other gown.

'Either would do very well,' Robert pronounced, 'but I prefer the first. I've always liked you in that.'

She stooped to kiss his forehead. 'That's settled then, that's the one I'll wear.' At that moment the front doorbell rang and Mrs Whiting left the kitchen to answer it, coming along to the sitting-room a minute or two later to say: 'It's Mrs Farrell. She'd like to come in for a few minutes but she'll quite understand if it's not convenient.' Lilian exchanged glances with Robert. He gave a little sigh, then he nodded and said: 'Show her in.'

When Bridget appeared in the doorway Lilian went forward with a welcoming smile. Robert remained seated. 'You must excuse the dressing-up,' Lilian said lightly. 'Robert's been helping me choose a dress for a charity dinner on Friday.'

'Are you going on your own?' Bridget asked.

'No, I'm going with the Joslins.' A quiet, amiable couple, the husband a local government official not far off retirement, his wife active in the charity hosting the dinner.

Bridget looked across at Robert who had now risen and came forward to greet her. 'I hope you don't mind me calling in like this,' she said apologetically. 'I came over to Cannonbridge straight from work, to see a friend in the hospital. I thought I'd take a chance and look in to ask how you were.' Her manner was placatory and ingratiating.

'We don't mind at all,' Robert reassured her, resolutely genial, and her face relaxed.

'I'll go and get out of this dress,' Lilian said. 'I'm afraid I have to be off out, I have a committee meeting. I expect you'd like something to eat if you came over straight from work. Mrs Whiting can easily get you something before she goes.'

Bridget shook her head. 'No, thanks, there's no need. I had something at the refreshment bar in the hospital, it will do me till I get home.'

'If you're sure,' Lilian said. She went quickly back up to her bedroom.

'We were both very sorry to hear about your illness,' Bridget told Robert when they were sitting down. 'But doctors are so clever now, I expect they'll soon have you feeling a lot better.

And there's research going on all the time. They're sure to find a cure one of these days.'

He didn't argue with her; he made a slight movement of his head in acknowledgement.

Neither of them made any direct mention of Keith nor did either refer in any way to the request for money and Robert's refusal. On the surface now it was as though that teatime conversation had never taken place.

Lilian came back a few minutes later, dressed in outdoor clothes. 'I'm sorry to run out on you like this,' she told Bridget.

'Don't worry about me,' Bridget returned airily. 'I'll stay and keep Uncle Robert company for a little while, if he'd like me to.'

Robert smiled without enthusiasm. 'You mustn't let me detain you. I know how busy you must be.'

She gave him back a cheerful smile. 'That's all right. I can spare the time. Nothing I'd like better.'

At the end of Friday morning Robert left Paragon to lunch at the golf club and play a round of golf afterwards. In the evening he ate his supper alone in the dining-room while Lilian was upstairs getting ready for the charity dinner. She was just about finished and was standing in her bedroom surveying herself in the mirror when the front doorbell rang. She heard Mrs Whiting go along to answer it and then, somewhat to her surprise, she heard Bridget Farrell's voice. Her face registered a degree of mild irritation followed by amused resignation. She left her bedroom and looked down over the banisters into the hall.

'Hello, there!' she called in friendly greeting. Mrs Whiting glanced up at her and went back to the kitchen.

'You do look lovely!' Bridget exclaimed and Lilian smiled in acknowledgement. 'I hope you don't mind me calling again so soon,' Bridget went on. 'I had the afternoon off and I came over to Cannonbridge to do some shopping and see my friend in hospital again.' She added hastily: 'You don't have to worry about me, I had something to eat while I was there. I called in to bring you a little present.' She took a confectioner's bag from her holdall. 'I saw these while I was shopping and I thought you might like them.'

61

'That's very kind of you,' Lilian answered, summoning up a show of appreciation. 'Hold on a moment. I'll just get my things and then I'll come down and join you.' She went back into her bedroom to pick up her wrap and evening bag. She gave a final glance into the mirror and went down into the hall.

Bridget drew a box from the bag and handed it to Lilian. 'Marrons glacés!' Lilian exclaimed. 'What a delightful surprise! Thank you so much!'

'I hoped you would like them,' Bridget responded eagerly.

'Oh, I do!' Lilian assured her with a good deal less than total truth. She opened the box and held it out. 'Do have one.' Bridget took one, unwrapped it and popped it in her mouth. 'I'd better not start on them myself,' Lilian said. 'I have a long dinner ahead of me.' She smiled. 'But I'll make up for it tomorrow.'

She took Bridget along to the sitting-room where Robert was now ensconced. 'Don't disturb yourself,' she told him. 'Look what Bridget's been kind enough to bring me: marrons glacés.' She held out the box. 'Would you like one?'

'Thank you, but I won't, not just now.' Robert had had little appetite for supper and wasn't in any case overfond of the taste of chestnuts.

Lilian offered the box again to Bridget who shook her head. 'I didn't buy them to eat them all myself,' she said lightly.

Lilian smiled. 'I'm sure Mrs Whiting would like one. Do sit down, Bridget.' She went off and found Mrs Whiting putting on her coat, about to leave. She proffered the marrons and Hester took one with lively interest. 'I've never eaten one of these before,' she explained as she removed the wrapper. 'Mm, it's certainly different,' she pronounced after some moments.

'Take another,' Lilian pressed her.

'Oh no, thank you, one will do me nicely.' She hadn't in fact been at all taken with the one she'd just eaten.

She expressed the hope that Lilian would enjoy the charity dinner; she said good-night and took herself off. Lilian went back to the sitting-room and put the box of marrons on top of a small cabinet. Bridget was chatting with animation to Robert about various items in the news, taking particular care to make herself agreeable.

Lilian asked Robert if he had all he might need for the rest of the evening.

'You mustn't worry about Uncle Robert,' Bridget put in solicitously. 'I'll stop on here a little longer, I'll look after him, keep him company.' Lilian exchanged covert glances with Robert, wryly amused. 'I'll probably go along to the study for a while before I go to bed,' he told her.

'I won't be too late back,' she assured him. 'The Joslins won't want to stay late. I'll probably be back around eleven fifteen, eleven thirty. I'll look in on you then.'

'I'll be sound asleep long before then,' he replied.

She smiled. 'I'll look in all the same. I'll be very quiet, I won't disturb you.'

'You'd have a job to do that,' he rejoined lightly. He added to Bridget: 'I sleep like a log with these pills I've got. They're first-class. They give you a sound night's sleep but they don't leave you feeling dopey next day.'

The front doorbell rang. 'That'll be the Joslins,' Lilian exclaimed. She went off to admit them and brought them along to have a word with Robert and be introduced to Bridget.

Robert went with them to the front door when they left. The evening was dry but overcast, with a chill in the air. 'Enjoy yourself,' he said to Lilian. He kissed her lovingly on the cheek, gave her shoulders an affectionate squeeze.

'I will.' She smiled tenderly up at him.

He came out on to the doorstep and stood watching as the three of them got into the Joslins' car. He didn't move until they had driven out through the gate, then he stepped back inside and closed the door.

The charity dinner was an undeniable success, the food delicious, the wines excellent, the company agreeable and stimulating, the speeches informative, amusing and not overlong. Lilian acquitted herself well, showing no sign of nervousness as she rose to speak.

She kept a watchful eye on the time as the evening wore on and at eleven she went with Mrs Joslin to retrieve their wraps from the cloakroom before following Joslin out to his car. The three of them chatted about the evening on the way back to Kincraig. Lilian had recently received a copy of the annual report of another charity in which Mrs Joslin was expressing an interest; she told Lilian now she would like to read the report.

'I've got it upstairs in my study,' Lilian said. 'I'll pop up for it, you can take it home with you. There's no rush to let me have it back.'

They turned in through the Kincraig gates. The house stood dark and silent. Lilian took the Joslins into the sitting-room. 'I won't be a moment,' she said as she laid her wrap over a chair. 'Make yourselves at home. I'll just look in on Robert before I get the report, then I'll make some coffee.' She left the room and the Joslins began to comment on the events of the evening.

Suddenly from upstairs there came a terrible, heart-stopping scream. They froze for an instant, then Joslin went swiftly from the room and up the stairs, followed, as fast as she could manage, by his wife.

The door of Robert's bedroom stood open, the low sound of music from a radio floated out. Joslin reached the threshold and took in the scene at a glance, in the subdued light of the bedside lamp.

Robert lay in bed, on his back, in a position of ease, the covers and pillows neatly disposed. Lilian was bending over him, her face contorted; she was tearing a clear plastic bag from over his head. A man's long white silk evening scarf had been thrown on top of the covers, half-way down the bed. Joslin ran up to Lilian. 'Allow me,' he said urgently. He laid two fingers against Robert's neck but could find no pulse.

'Is he dead?' Lilian cried.

Joslin didn't answer that. He turned his head and called out to his wife who had now reached the doorway and stood looking in, appalled. 'Get an ambulance!' he instructed. 'And his doctor.' He flung a command at Lilian: 'Go with her. You can do nothing here.' She ran from the room.

Joslin began at once to administer the mouth-to-mouth resuscitation he had learned at first-aid classes and had never until this moment had occasion to employ. On the bedside table the radio played its soothing music. Beside it stood a large cup and saucer, with a teaspoon. Next to them were two small bottles, one holding tablets, the other capsules. Protruding from underneath the radio was a folded cutting from a glossy magazine.

13

In the early hours of Saturday morning Detective Chief Inspector Kelsey, accompanied by Detective Sergeant Lambert, came out of the front door of Kincraig and walked down the drive to where they had left the car, near the gate. The Chief was a big, solidly built man with a head of thickly springing carroty hair, shrewd green eyes, craggy features, a freckled face dominated by a large squashy nose. He had had some slight acquaintance with Robert Anstey, who had come across as a quiet, exceptionally hardworking, purposeful man of great integrity, a good employer, well regarded locally. Kelsey had never actually met Lilian Anstey before, though he had known who she was and had seen her at various functions.

Anstey's body had gone to the mortuary; the post-mortem would begin later in the morning. Lilian Anstey had only just retired to her bedroom. She had recovered control of herself early on and had not again given way openly to shock and grief. Kelsey had asked if there was any relative of herself or her husband living locally, that she would like them to contact. But it appeared that she had no one in the area and the only relative of her husband's – or rather, of his first wife – that she knew of anywhere at all was a niece of that wife, a Mrs Bridget Farrell, living in Wychford. She explained that Bridget had looked in at Kincraig earlier that evening and had still been in the house when Lilian had left with the Joslins; she had said she would be staying a little longer.

Kelsey had expressed a wish to speak to Mrs Farrell, who might be able to shed some light on Anstey's state of mind. Lilian told him she would be phoning Bridget first thing in the morning, before she might chance to learn what had happened from the local radio or some other source. She was sure Bridget would wish to come over. Kelsey said he would be returning to Kincraig in the early afternoon to give Lilian the post-mortem findings; he would be glad if she could arrange for him to talk to Mrs Farrell then.

Dr Thornley had pronounced life extinct at eleven forty. His estimate for the time of death was between one and two hours earlier. There was no letter but in Thornley's opinion it was a clear case of suicide. Anyone choosing to use that method, not at all a common one, struck him as being pretty determined to die. Anstey knew his wife wouldn't be home before eleven, he could have had no expectation of being discovered in time to be revived; death would have come too soon for that to be feasible.

Thornley told Kelsey of the recent diagnosis of Anstey's illness, the grim outlook for the future. 'It must have come as a savage blow to him,' he said with a melancholy shake of his head. 'He always prided himself on being fit, taking good care of his health. He told me more than once that he had every intention of living to over a hundred – and he wasn't joking.'

He drew a long sigh. 'I thought he was coming to terms with his illness but I believe now he'd made up his mind from the start what he was going to do.' Anstey hadn't been a man to relish the prospect of a long decline. He had never mentioned the possibility of suicide to Thornley and the doctor had never considered it a danger. But he realized now just how much Anstey must have detested the notion of becoming increasingly dependent and the certain prospect of his brain being affected in the later stages. He was certainly a man who could make tough decisions and stick to them. And he liked to play his cards close to his chest.

He indicated the folded cutting they had found underneath the radio: a page from the magazine supplement of one of the Ansteys' regular Sunday newspapers; it had been taken from a recent issue. Lilian had no recollection of her husband having made any comment about the article or indeed of having read the article herself.

It was part of a feature dealing with the campaign for legalized euthanasia, setting out arguments for and against, the current state of legislation and opinion in various countries. The article included an interview with one of the most vocal advocates of legal euthanasia. He outlined the difficulties at present facing a terminally ill patient wishing to end his own life. He stated categorically that the only reliable method open to such a person without medical assistance was self-asphyxiation by the use of a plastic bag. He described the method in detail, advising the taking, shortly beforehand, of a large enough dose of sleeping pills to induce speedy drowsiness.

Lilian managed only a succession of fitful dozes during the remainder of the night. She was up again early to ring both Hester Whiting and the Farrells.

As Hester took in the news she could barely speak for shock. When she did find her voice she assured Lilian, unasked, that she would be along without delay, she would do all in her power to help.

When the news was broken to Bridget Farrell she began to cry before Lilian had finished speaking. When she had regained a measure of control she said in a shaking voice: 'We can't either of us come over right away, we're both working this morning. But we could come this afternoon, if you'd like us to.'

'Indeed I would,' Lilian responded warmly. 'Mrs Whiting will be here shortly.' She explained that Chief Inspector Kelsey would like a word with Bridget. 'He'll be here this afternoon,' she added, 'so he can talk to you then.'

Dr Thornley arrived at the hospital for the final stages of the post-mortem. When it was over he left the building with Chief Inspector Kelsey.

The post-mortem had revealed nothing that in any way quarrelled with the notion of suicide. The toxicology report would not be to hand for a few days but there could be little doubt about the cause of death.

'Something I remembered on my way here,' the doctor said as they crossed the car-park. 'I had a patient who died five or six years ago, he was retired, about seventy-five. He'd worked for Paragon for years, he'd been a foreman. He had a stroke, a pretty bad one, and when he was able to communicate again, after a fashion, he asked me about the future, what was the best he could hope for. He insisted on the truth. He was a widower, no children, no relatives, living on his own. He'd had an active retirement, liked to get out and about, a bit of fishing, gardening, going to football and cricket matches, a drink at the pub. He'd never been one to sit reading a book, listening to the radio, watching TV. And he wasn't a religious man.

'I gave him as optimistic a picture as I could: he would always need to live in care of some sort, he might hope in time to progress to a wheelchair.

'He thanked me, he made no comment. From that day he refused all food and drink, all medication, all treatment. It took him a week to die.' He paused. 'What came back to me this morning was something I remembered Robert Anstey saying when I told him of the man's death. He said: "He was always a man of character. I'd like to think I'd have the guts to do what he did if I ever found myself in the same situation."'

The Farrells hadn't yet arrived when Kelsey called at Kincraig shortly after lunch. He found Lilian composed, although she looked pale and heavy-eyed. She listened in silence to what he had to tell her about the post-mortem. When he went on to ask her one or two questions about her husband she was able to answer readily, without open distress.

Had her husband carried much life insurance?

She shook her head. As far as she knew, he carried none at all.

Did she know of any pressing business worries?

She replied that the business was flourishing, continuing to expand. Robert did have one matter troubling him. She gave the Chief a brief outline of the fraud investigation and the suspension of Matthew Shardlow. But she couldn't call it a major worry, certainly not weighty enough to prey on Robert's mind or cause serious depression. She clasped her hands, she looked weary and strained. 'I thought he was coming to terms with his illness.' He had taken his medicines faithfully, had scrupulously followed medical instructions. He had cut down at work, had withdrawn from tiring social engagements. He had, it was true, been very quiet since the diagnosis but she had thought that only to be expected. He had never talked of suicide but neither, as she now realized, had he spoken to any extent of the future. 'There were days when I could see he felt low but I had no idea –' She broke off and sat with her head lowered.

When the Farrells arrived a few minutes later Lilian let Mrs Whiting go home, to attend belatedly to her own chores and weekend shopping. The Chief had a word with Bridget on her own. She told him she had stayed a mere ten minutes with Uncle Robert after Lilian had left with the Joslins. His manner during that time was in no way out of the ordinary. She had had not the slightest inkling of what was in his mind but it was clear to her now that suicide must all along have been a possibility. If he preferred a swift and painless death to the bleak alternative, that had been his choice and one must respect that.

Officers who went along to the golf club on Sunday morning were able to speak to the members Robert had met on Friday. It seemed he had said nothing to anyone to give any indication of what was in his mind. He had certainly seemed quiet but not to an extent that caused any comment. His death and the manner of it had come as a great shock. They had known nothing of his illness; he had merely let it be known a week or two earlier that he would be playing golf two afternoons a week in future, on doctor's orders. They had accepted that without question, knowing him to be an exceptionally hard worker; it wasn't surprising if the doctor had told a man of his age he should start to slacken off, relax more, get more exercise in the fresh air.

According to British Telecom, only one phone call had been made from Kincraig after seven thirty on Friday evening. The call, made at nine fifteen and lasting a little over five minutes, had been made to a number registered in the name of Stephen Hibberd, in a town some forty-five miles from Cannonbridge.

Early on Sunday afternoon Sergeant Lambert drove Chief Inspector Kelsey over there, through the bright autumn weather. The address took them to a trim semi on the outskirts of town.

Two small children were playing in the front garden under the supervision of a motherly-looking woman in late middle age. When the car pulled up and the two men got out and approached the gate she gave them a glance of friendly inquiry. The Chief introduced himself and told her they were looking for a Mr Stephen Hibberd, in the hope that he might be able to help them with some information.

She didn't appear at all perturbed; she seemed a pleasant

69

woman, not easily flustered. 'Stephen's my son-in-law,' she answered amiably. Her name was Mrs Vine. 'My daughter's inside, in the kitchen. Stephen's round the back, tidying up the garden. Go on round and have a word with him.'

They found Hibberd clearing the vegetable beds. 'You'd better come inside,' he responded when the Chief had again said his piece. As he took the two men indoors his wife put her head out of the kitchen and Hibberd made the introductions. She looked keenly interested when he explained that the Chief was in search of information and asked if she might join them.

'Come along by all means,' Kelsey invited.

In the living-room Kelsey asked if Hibberd had received a phone call from Cannonbridge at nine fifteen on Friday evening.

'Yes, I did,' Hibberd replied at once. 'It was from Mr Anstey – he owns Paragon Tools.'

'Were you expecting the call?' Kelsey inquired.

Hibberd shook his head. 'I went over to Paragon about a month ago to see if I could get on their list of suppliers, making handles. I have a woodturning business. Mr Anstey liked my samples and my prices but he didn't have a vacancy just then. He said he'd be in touch as soon as there was an opening. That was what the phone call was about. He rang to say they did have an opening now.'

Kelsey asked if either of them had listened to any of the day's news bulletins, or those of the previous day, on local radio.

They both shook their heads. Hibberd frowned in sudden concern. 'Is there something wrong with Paragon?' he asked on a note of sharp anxiety.

'There's nothing at all wrong with them, to the best of my knowledge,' Kelsey assured him. A look of profound relief flashed across Hibberd's features. 'But I'm sorry to have to tell you there's bad news about Mr Anstey.' Both heads jerked up. Again a look of acute anxiety on Hibberd's face. 'I'm afraid he's dead,' Kelsey went on. Nell gave a gasp. 'He died on Friday evening.'

Silence fell over the room.

'Friday evening?' Hibberd echoed. 'What time was that?' His voice was appalled, astounded.

'Difficult to be exact at this stage,' Kelsey answered. 'Probably fairly late in the evening.'

'How did he die?'

There was a perceptible pause before Kelsey answered: 'He died from asphyxia. He had a plastic bag over his head.'

In the horrified silence Nell began to weep. She took out a handkerchief, dabbed at her eyes, sat with her head lowered.

'Why would he want to kill himself?' Hibberd's voice shook. 'Was he in trouble? Did he leave a letter?'

Kelsey didn't answer any of that. 'You can see now why we're here. We'd like you to think back over that phone call, try to remember everything that was said.'

Nell's weeping stopped abruptly. She directed a piercing gaze at Kelsey. 'If Mr Anstey's dead, does that mean there's no contract? Nothing's been signed, there's nothing legal.'

Kelsey moved his head. 'I wouldn't know about any of that. I imagine it'll be up to whoever will be running Paragon now.' He repeated his request for Hibberd to think back over the phone call.

Hibberd appeared visibly shaken but he closed his eyes in an attempt at concentrated thought. 'He said there was a vacancy now on his list.' His voice was unsteady. 'He would be offering me a contract. I jumped at it. I thanked him, said it was wonderful news, I'd make sure he never had reason to regret it. He said he was going away but he'd spoken to his wife and she would be putting the contract through right away. He'd decided to give me a ring, tell me the news himself before he went. If I had any queries I should get in touch with his wife on Monday morning.' He came to a halt and opened his eyes.

'Was anything else said?' Kelsey asked. 'Anything at all?'

Again Hibberd thought back. 'When he said he'd decided to give me a ring before he went, he said he always liked to leave things tied up, no loose ends.'

'How did he sound?'

'Businesslike. Friendly. He certainly didn't sound depressed or agitated.'

Kelsey asked Nell Hibberd if she had been present during the phone call.

She shook her head. 'I was in the kitchen with my mother, she spent the evening here. I heard the phone go and a few minutes later Stephen came running into the kitchen. He was over the moon, he told us about the contract. We were all absolutely

71

delighted.' She jerked her head in the direction of the garden. 'You can speak to my mother now, if you like.'

'Yes, I would like a word with her,' Kelsey said.

She got to her feet. 'I'll go and tell her. I'll stay out with the children while she's in here.' She went off and a few minutes later Mrs Vine came into the room. Judging by her manner, as pleasantly composed as before, Kelsey guessed that Nell had made no mention to her of Anstey's death.

He asked what she could tell him of an incoming phone call on Friday evening. She had no difficulty in recalling it and her recollection squared with what her daughter had just told them.

Before they left, the Chief told Hibberd it was possible he could be called to give evidence at the inquest, but that wasn't likely to be just yet. The inquest would be opened and in all likelihood adjourned, one day next week, but it would only be at the resumed inquest, probably a week or two later, that he would be called, if at all. Hibberd gave a nod of acquiescence.

On the way back to the police station they called in at Kincraig. Lilian still looked pale and heavy-eyed, though her manner was still tightly controlled.

Yes, she did know the name Stephen Hibberd; he owned a small manufacturing firm in the county. Robert had told her at lunch-time on Friday, as he was leaving for the golf club, that he had decided to give Hibberd a contract. He asked her to see to it on Monday morning.

Kelsey asked if Robert had intended making a trip of some sort but she shook her head; she was positive there had been no trip in the offing.

'I'll see to the contract on Monday, as Robert asked me to,' she said after a moment. 'He wouldn't have wanted Hibberd worrying over whether the contract would go ahead. Robert never forgot his own early days, he knew what it was like to struggle along from one week to the next.'

14

On Monday morning Kelsey had a word with Robert Anstey's solicitor. Cartwright told him the terms of Anstey's will, adding

72

that Bridget Farrell had stood to inherit the bulk of the estate under Anstey's previous will, though she had never been informed of that. He confirmed that Robert had carried no life insurance. 'He never took out any life policy at any time, not as a young man starting out and not during his first marriage. He had strong views on the subject. He took the attitude that he had every intention of living to a ripe old age and he could invest his spare cash more effectively than any insurance company.' Anstey was far from being in any kind of financial difficulty and Paragon was doing well.

He had last seen Anstey when he came to the office to discuss the matter of the fraud investigation. Cartwright's advice had been the same as Lilian's: don't bring a case against Matthew Shardlow, however much you're tempted. Bite the bullet, pay him off, then put the whole thing behind you.

Anstey had phoned the office while Cartwright was on holiday; he had told Cartwright's secretary he would phone again after Cartwright returned. But he hadn't done so – Cartwright had been back at his desk five days when Anstey died.

Kelsey asked to speak to the secretary and Sylvie Murchison was summoned, a middle-aged woman, neatly and plainly dressed, a severe hairstyle, no make-up; she looked a serious, dedicated worker. She took a seat, perching herself bolt upright on the edge of her chair.

She answered the Chief's questions without hesitation, giving them her full attention. Mr Anstey had rung first thing on the Monday morning – 30th September, that would be. She didn't get the impression it was anything important or urgent. He said he wanted to discuss possible changes in his will. No, he had in no way indicated what the changes might be.

Her right hand rested on her left forearm; all the time she talked, the fingers of her right hand moved ceaselessly and unobtrusively, plucking at the sleeve of her tailored jacket.

In the afternoon Kelsey talked briefly to the auditors handling the fraud investigation. He was told that the inquiry was almost completed and it was their firm belief that now that Anstey was dead no case would come before the courts.

The Chief then spoke to Lilian in her office at Paragon. She looked a good deal more like her old self, livelier and less distressed. It was clearly much better for her to be compelled to give her mind to the complex demands of the business, to be allowed little time to dwell on the sorrows of her personal situation.

She told the Chief everyone at Paragon was being helpful and supportive. As to the fraud investigation, she definitely had no wish for any case to be brought against Shardlow. That had been her view from the first and Robert had always known it.

Kelsey asked if she knew why Robert had rung his solicitor on Monday, 30th September. Yes, she replied at once, she did know. She gave him a brief outline of the Farrells' teatime visit to Kincraig on the Sunday, their request to Robert for an advance on Bridget's legacy, Robert's dismissive response, his discussion of the matter with her over supper. 'He said he would speak to Cartwright, to see if he could attach some conditions to Bridget's legacy to make it difficult for her husband to get his hands on it.' She smiled slightly. 'I told him I thought he was over-reacting. He didn't mention it to me again and I came to the conclusion he'd had second thoughts and decided there was no good reason after all to change his will.'

The inquest on Robert James Anstey was opened on Wednesday morning and adjourned a few minutes later, as the Chief had expected, no date being set for resumption.

Late the following afternoon the Chief received the toxicology report. Nothing in it was at variance with the presumption of suicide. Anstey had, it appeared, taken sufficient sleeping pills to ensure that he very quickly fell into a profound sleep. There was also in his stomach a single undissolved capsule, one of those he had been prescribed as part of the treatment of his illness.

Kelsey sat for some time reviewing the circumstances of Anstey's death. He was satisfied that a verdict of suicide would be returned and would be fully justified. He decided to call in at Kincraig on his way home to let Lilian know the gist of the report and to tell her the investigation was now concluded and a day could be set for the resumed inquest. He would see to that tomorrow and would then give her a ring to let her know the date and time, most probably in a week or so.

He felt a lightening of his spirits. It was always good to be able to draw a line under a case. He got to his feet and crossed to the window, he stood looking out at the peaceful sky. Tonight was Hallowe'en and might turn out lively enough, but that shouldn't bother him. He was looking forward to the luxury of a restful evening, a long, sound night's sleep.

15

At nine thirty on Friday evening, in a rural spot half a mile from the nearest village and some five miles from Cannonbridge, two lads of thirteen from neighbouring families living in cottages that had at one time housed farmworkers, set off to walk their dogs, as they usually did around this time. They liked to vary the direction of their walk and this evening chose a road they hadn't followed for a week or two. It carried little traffic and led them away from the village towards a stretch of woodland known as Crowswood.

The air was chilly. The moon shone down from a sky bright with stars. When they neared the wood they unclipped the leads and the dogs ran free, sniffing delightedly, frisking back and forth, up a slope and down again.

One of the dogs raced ahead, down an incline; he sniffed about in the bracken, the tangles of bramble, drifts of copper leaves, roots and stones, moving in on the undergrowth beneath an overhanging boulder sheltered by low branches. He began to bark loudly. The other dog abandoned his own exploring and chased after him. In a few moments he too was scratching and yapping, the two of them out of sight of the boys who were deep in conversation about their plans for the weekend.

The barking persisted, grew louder and more excited, breaking into the lads' talk. They halted and glanced down the incline at the shadowy patch some yards away where the dogs bayed and scrabbled. One lad uttered an exclamation and began to make his way swiftly down the slope. His friend followed him.

They reached the spot where the dogs kept up their clamour, their working. The rays of the moon struck through the branches, revealing among the brambles and clumps of old grass the lower half of a leg. A child's leg, clad in jeans, the foot encased in a black trainer.

The lads fell to their knees and began to tear at the brushwood and bracken, uncovering within a few minutes the rest of the body: a young boy, slight and short, with cropped fair hair, lying face down, wearing a casual jacket.

The night was fine and calm, no threat of rain. In the early hours of Saturday morning Chief Inspector Kelsey and Sergeant Lambert made their way back up the slope towards their car. The body had gone to the mortuary. A painstaking search of the site would begin at first light.

The boy had plainly been dead for some time; the pathologist's present estimate could be no more exact than a guess at six to eight days. An examination of the insect life would help to establish the time more closely.

It was equally plain that the death had taken place elsewhere, the body being taken some hours later to the spot where it was found. There was no disturbance of the clothing to suggest a sex motive, no sign of any struggle.

The boy had died from strangulation by a hand applied with considerable force. Perceptible showers of haemorrhages on the face showed that the grasp had been maintained for several seconds past the point at which the child would have lost consciousness, clearly indicating a determined intention to kill.

In the right-hand pocket of the boy's jacket was a crumpled handkerchief; underneath it, a small plastic torch. In the left-hand pocket there were three sprigs of different flowering shrubs, still bearing faint traces of scent. In the same pocket was a small square of decorative gold-coloured foil, neatly folded in four. In the left-hand breast pocket was a tube of medicated lozenges, three-quarters full.

Some silky-looking threads had been caught up on the Velcro fastening strip of one of the boy's trainers, on the teeth of an open zip fastener on one of the pockets of his jacket and on the teeth of the jacket front zip, which had been only partly closed. It looked to Kelsey as if the threads could have come from something used to wrap the body before conveying it to where it was to lie concealed.

A name appeared on the boy's clothing, printed in ink, in block capitals, on the labels of both his jacket and his trainers. The name had been carefully set down in full: WILLIAM EDWARD COLEMAN.

Kelsey was able to snatch a few hours' sleep before the work of identifying the body could begin in earnest. As soon as it was judged a fitting hour to rouse folk from sleep a couple of detective constables began the task of telephoning the head teachers of all the primary schools in the area. One of the constables soon struck lucky. The headmaster of a Cannonbridge school, near the Westway council estate, recognized the name as belonging to one of his pupils. Yes, he could see the constable right away. And yes, he would immediately ring the boy's class teacher and have her join them.

The headmaster, hastily dressed, unshaved, was standing on the doorstep a few minutes later, looking out for the constable. He left the front door ajar for the class teacher and took the constable along to the sitting-room, walking quietly, speaking in low tones, the rest of the household being still in bed. The class teacher, always an early riser, turned up a few minutes later, neatly groomed and dressed for the day. She was a sensible-looking woman in her early forties, experienced and level-headed.

William Edward Coleman – Billy Coleman, as they knew him – was, it appeared, ten years old. His mother was dead, his father working abroad. There were no other children. He lived with his stepmother on the Westway estate. He was a quiet lad, well behaved, above average in intelligence. He worked hard at school and was anxious to get on. 'I think he tended to romanticize the past,' the class teacher said. 'It came through when he wrote a story or a composition. He seemed to look back on a golden age when his Mum and Dad were both there.'

He attended school regularly and punctually, was always clean and tidy. He had never been in trouble in the school. He didn't have many friends but neither did he have any enemies. The class teacher knew of one good friend named David Willcox, in the same class, also living on the Westway estate. 'But I don't know that David's going to be able to help you very much,' she added. 'He's in hospital at present, he's been away from school for over two weeks.'

Billy had not been in school for the past week. He had attended as usual on the Friday before the half-term holiday, 18th October. He had seemed much as usual. When he didn't turn up for school after the holiday, on Monday, 28th October, she asked the class if anyone knew why he was absent, but no one knew. The school was hot on truancy and when Billy failed to show up again the following day she called round to his house on her way home at the end of the afternoon.

No one answered her rings and knocks; the house looked closed up. She went next door but found no one at home. After trying at the next pair of semis, with no better luck, she gave up and went home.

When Billy still hadn't shown up at school by the Thursday morning she decided to call round to his house again, this time during the lunch hour. Again she got no reply but a woman going by recognized the teacher, saw her failure to get any response. 'You won't find anyone there,' she called out. When the teacher joined her at the gate, the woman told her: 'Mrs Coleman's gone off with one of her boyfriends. I saw them putting cases in the car. They'll have gone on holiday.' Billy hadn't gone with them, she was sure of that. She had watched the car drive off and there'd been no sign of Billy. She hadn't seen him for some days. She guessed he might have gone off later to join the other two or he might be staying with some friend or relative. She made a face. 'Or he may just have taken off, he could be roaming about, enjoying himself, till they get back.'

The teacher asked her class that afternoon if anyone knew if Billy had gone on holiday but again, no one knew. She decided he would probably turn up before long and she let the matter rest there.

By eight o'clock the first house-to-house teams were active in both the Westway and Crowswood areas. A call at the Coleman house received no response but the police learned from neighbours the name of the club where Mrs Coleman worked. The club was known to the police as a well-run establishment; the owner, a middle-aged man by the name of Yates, took care to keep on the right side of the law. A detective constable was dispatched to talk to him at his home.

Yates was appalled to learn of the death of Mrs Coleman's stepson. He knew nothing of the circumstances in which, it appeared, Billy had been left to fend for himself. He told the constable that Mrs Coleman had had two weeks' leave owing to her and she had arranged at fairly short notice to take the last two weeks in October; she was due to return to work next Monday, 4th November.

He didn't know how she had proposed to spend the two weeks, nor had she said anything about her stepson in this respect. She was never one to volunteer personal information and he had never poked his nose into the private lives of his staff.

He believed Mrs Coleman was friendly with another member of staff, Mrs Edna Quirke. Edna was a widow, employed in the club kitchen; he would put her at some fifteen years older than Mrs Coleman. She wasn't due to come into work today until after lunch. He gave the constable her address: a cottage on the outskirts of Cannonbridge.

The constable found Edna on the point of driving into Cannonbridge to do her weekend shopping. She hadn't been listening to the local radio, she knew nothing of what had happened. She was overcome at the news and took some minutes to recover sufficiently to answer questions. Not that she had known Billy well. Mrs Coleman – Glenna, as she called her – had never talked of him much, but from the few times Edna had spoken to the lad she had thought him quiet and well behaved.

She was able to shed a little light on where Glenna might be now. Glenna had told her she was going to a caravan on the south coast; she had been no more specific than that. She hadn't said for how long and Edna hadn't asked; she had taken it for granted it would be for the whole two weeks. She was going with Lew Dutton, a man she had been friendly with for a month or two. She hadn't mentioned Billy and it hadn't occurred to Edna to ask if he would be going too. If she had thought about it at all she would have assumed Billy would be going with them or if not, that proper arrangements would have been made. Certainly Glenna hadn't asked her to keep an eye on the lad or anything of that sort. She confidently expected Glenna back at work on Monday.

She couldn't say that she and Glenna were particularly close, merely that she was closer to Glenna than any other member of staff. She had known Glenna for eighteen months, since Glenna started working at the club. She had never laid eyes on Glenna's husband. All she knew of him was that he was working abroad somewhere and that as far as Glenna was concerned the marriage would appear to be over, though Glenna never spoke of divorce or indeed of any plans for the future. She was never very forthcoming about her private life and Edna was never inclined to ask questions.

Before Glenna took up with Lew Dutton she had been friendly with another man by the name of Tom Palmer; Glenna had met both men at the club. Palmer was better looking and better off than Dutton but it seemed he was inclined to drink more than was good for him and could be free with his fists when in drink. He and Glenna had been quite thick for a time and then she broke off with him.

She couldn't supply the address of either Dutton or Palmer nor did she know where either man worked but she was sure those facts would be known to some of the regulars at the club.

The teams covering the Crowswood area had so far come up with nothing at all. No one had seen or heard any unusual activity; no one knew anything of the boy or his family. But on the Westway estate the teams continued to amass driblets of information, rumour, guesswork and gossip about the Colemans' marriage, Glenna's way of life, her attitude to Billy. A woman living a few doors away told them this wasn't the first time Glenna had gone off, leaving Billy on his own. 'If she'd come back from one of her jaunts and found he'd run off for good,' she added grimly, 'it's my belief she'd have been delighted to be rid of a burden.'

They found a man in the same road who was slightly acquainted with Lew Dutton, able to tell them where he lived: with his older sister and her husband, a Mr and Mrs Reeve, in a block of council flats a quarter of a mile away. A call at the flat produced no response but a woman in the flat opposite told them the Reeves had gone to a newly opened shopping mall in a nearby town. They intended lunching out and wouldn't be back before the early afternoon.

The teams also learned of various sightings of Billy during the half-term holiday, none of them particularly enlightening. The latest sighting they could discover was at around five thirty on the evening of Friday, 25th October, when Billy had visited the corner shop, a few minutes' walk from home.

The shopkeeper's wife told them Billy had called in daily over the half-term break, making purchases of convenience foods, confectionery, soft drinks and the like. He had said nothing about being on his own in the house, but he had never been a lad to chat while he was in the shop; he gave his full attention to selecting his purchases, reckoning up his money. He was always well behaved, never light-fingered.

Asked if she could recall anything in any way different about him on his last visit, all she could come up with was that he was starting a cold. He had asked if she had any throat sweets and she had sold him some medicated lozenges.

Could she recall precisely what else he had bought on this last visit?

She told them he had bought much the same items every day: a small pork pie, a packet of crisps, a choc-ice and a can of soft drink, plus one or two extras that varied from day to day. She rather thought he had bought a box of little fancy cakes that Friday.

One thing her husband had particularly noticed. The Colemans never had any papers delivered nor did Glenna ever buy a newspaper at the shop, but Billy always bought a football magazine, the same one every week. A copy was always put by for him and he always called in for it without fail on Saturday morning, usually around nine o'clock. But he hadn't called in for it last Saturday, 26th October. The shopkeeper showed the officers the copy, still waiting on a back shelf, marked with the name Coleman, together with the latest copy, laid aside for Billy only this morning.

The house where Billy's schoolfriend, David Willcox, lived was situated in the most respectable part of the estate. David's mother answered the door to the police team. In common with the rest of the estate she now knew of Billy's death. Her main response to the news appeared to be a determination to prevent the horrifying event in any way affecting the well-being or good name of her son. She grudgingly conceded that the two boys may have been friendly at one time but hastened to point out that she had never encouraged the association. She was firmly of the opinion that the friendship had withered some time back. Billy's background had struck her as undesirable and she had never allowed David to frequent that part of the estate.

As to the police wishing to speak to David, she couldn't see what he could possibly tell them. He couldn't even have laid eyes on Billy for over a fortnight. He had been in hospital for more than a week and had been ill at home for over a week before that. He had had influenza which had turned to acute bronchitis, threatening pneumonia. The worst of it was now over and he had reached the convalescent stage. She would be going to the hospital this afternoon and again, with her husband, tomorrow. They hoped to be told then that they could bring David home on Monday afternoon. They would say nothing to him while he was in hospital about what had happened to Billy and she had already given strict instructions to the hospital that the news was to be kept from him. If he was discharged on Monday she must insist he had the night to settle in and then, if the police still felt it essential to talk to him, they could do so on Tuesday morning. She gave her word to say nothing before-hand of what had happened.

The name of Ormerod, the Colemans' neighbour, cropped up several times in the course of the Westway inquiries. It was invariably a youngster who recounted with relish the episode of Ormerod's dog, the youngster in every case loudly maintaining his own total innocence of any involvement in the torment-ing and killing of the creature. The story was always the same: Billy had had nothing to do with the ill-treatment of the animal but Ormerod had always refused to accept that. It was well known that Billy made a point of keeping out of Ormerod's way and it was generally held that in this he showed good sense.

Officers calling at Ormerod's house got no response. Neighbours said he would be at work, he would probably be back at lunch-time.

When the police effected an entry into the Colemans' house they found no indication of struggle or disturbance. All was neat and tidy, with the exception of what was clearly Glenna's bedroom, where a certain amount of what seemed habitual disorder reigned.

In the kitchen they found a box of small fancy cakes identical with that shown to them in the shop but with two cakes missing. In the pedal bin they found an empty soft-drink can, wrappers from a pork pie and choc-ice and an empty crisps packet. In one of the kitchen cupboards was a jar holding five-pound notes.

In Billy's bedroom it didn't take them long to discover the box containing the money and photograph. But nowhere in the house could they come upon any article likely to have been the source of the silky threads caught up in the zip fasteners and Velcro strip of Billy's clothing. It had now been established that the threads were of pure silk, grey in colour.

The small six-year-old car standing in the garage corresponded with the description the neighbours had given them of Glenna's car. After a superficial inspection yielding nothing of significance the vehicle was removed for more thorough examination.

An attempt was made to locate the whereabouts of Billy's father. A neighbour supplied the name of the firm that had employed him until eighteen months ago and contact was made with one of the firm's managers.

He could tell them little. Coleman had given no reason for leaving the firm nor did he say what his plans were. But the manager was able to give them the names and addresses of two men still with the firm who had worked in the same gang as Coleman.

The police found one of the men at home. He could tell them little more. He would describe Coleman as on the quiet side, not ill-tempered or aggressive. He had the impression that Coleman had left his job and his home because of difficulties in his marriage. He had been very cagey about his plans, understandable if he didn't want his wife to know where he was going. The workmate was pretty certain from one or two remarks Coleman had let slip that he had found a job abroad. He had never heard from Coleman after he left, nor had he had news of him from any source. Nor, to the best of his knowledge, had any others in the gang.

Checks showed that Coleman had no police record in England. An attempt would now be made to locate him in various countries abroad, using official channels: the police, immigration, labour ministries, as well as British embassies.

Before the start of the post-mortem the two teachers were asked if either of them would be willing to make an initial identification of the body as the police had been unable to contact any relatives. Neither had any objection and they decided to go together to the mortuary. In spite of believing themselves fully prepared for the ordeal, well steeled against its impact, they both found themselves severely shaken, reduced to tears.

A constable had earlier been dispatched to the county college of horticulture to gain what information he could about the sprigs of shrubs in Billy's pocket. While the post-mortem was still under way he returned to the station with positive identification of all three shrubs, together with colour photographs, details of habit, likely sites, flowering season and so forth.

Armed with the information and copies of the photographs, the house-to-house teams and all other officers on the case would be keeping their eyes open from now on for any of these shrubs, particularly for any instance of the three growing in close association.

At the end of the post-mortem Sergeant Lambert drove the Chief back to the station. The post-mortem had yielded no surprises. They would have to wait for a detailed analysis of the stomach contents and the insect life but all the facts amassed so far encouraged the belief that Billy could have met his death during the later part of Friday evening, 25th October.

There were no signs of any struggle: no torn nails or damaged cuticles; scrapings from beneath the nails had proved negative.

Nor was there any indication of sexual interference, either at around the time of death or at any time previously.

16

When officers made a lunch-time call on Ormerod they saw his van parked at the side of the house. He had just got in from work, he was upstairs in the bathroom, having a wash. He came down in answer to their ring; he stood drying his face and hands on a towel as they explained their mission.

Yes, he had heard the terrible news about Billy Coleman, he had heard it in the course of his morning's rounds. Yes, of course, he would be happy to answer any questions, tell them anything he knew.

He took them into a comfortable living-room, clean and tidy. He gave them his full name, told them where he worked – the scrapyard, they noted, was nowhere near Crowswood.

No, he had had no contact with Billy during the week of the half-term holiday. Yes, he had realized the lad was in the house on his own, he had seen Mrs Coleman drive off on the Friday with Lew Dutton, whom he knew by sight. No, he had felt no concern for the lad. Mrs Coleman had gone off before and left Billy on his own.

Wasn't it true that he had been on bad terms with Billy? Seeing Billy alone in the house, no one to protect him, had he not been tempted to have a go at the boy?

He shook his head vigorously. No, he had not been tempted. All that old business of the dog was water under the bridge, he'd put it behind him long ago. It didn't do to go brooding about things over and done with.

He went swiftly on to say he had seen someone call next door about twenty minutes after Mrs Coleman had driven off with Dutton. It was a man called Palmer, Tom Palmer. Again, Ormerod knew him by sight. He had been a frequent caller next door a few months back. He described the altercation with

Billy, the way Palmer had struck out at the boy and would doubtless have gone further had he not caught sight of Ormerod watching him.

No, he hadn't seen Palmer near the house again, after that call.

As the teams were now directing the main thrust of their inquiries at the events of Friday, 25th October, they asked if Ormerod could tell them how he had spent that evening.

He had no difficulty in replying: he had spent the evening as he spent every Friday evening, at the Plough and Harrow, in a village half a mile outside Cannonbridge – again, the officers noted, in a direction nowhere near Crowswood. The Plough and Harrow was his usual pub. He had long ago given up drinking at any pub near the Westway estate, with its prying eyes and wagging tongues. He called in at the Plough and Harrow one or two evenings most weeks and always on a Friday.

Had he seen anyone at all at or near the Colemans' house during the week of the half-term holiday?

No, he had seen no one but he had been particularly busy at work that week, getting back late most evenings.

Had he noticed if there were any lights on in the Colemans' house that Friday evening?

He couldn't recall, one way or the other. He had got in from work around six, washed and changed, gone straight along to the pub for a drink and something to eat.

He supplied, unasked, details of the make, colour and approximate age of the cars belonging to both Palmer and Dutton, adding that he didn't know the registration number of either.

Could he tell them Tom Palmer's address?

No, but he could tell them where Palmer worked.

When they went on to say they would be taking his van for forensic examination he sat for some moments without speaking, regarding them with a stunned air, then he roused himself to give a nod of acquiescence, adding that he would be greatly obliged if he could have the van back in time for work on Monday morning. They noted his request but could make no promises.

He looked even more stunned when they asked if they might look through his things. After a brief silence he indicated that he had no objection. He remained where he was while they went swiftly upstairs and down. Nowhere did they discover any article that might have supplied the grey silk threads.

As soon as they left Ormerod they went in search of Tom Palmer. One of the officers knew a foreman at the firm where Palmer worked. He was able to contact the man and was given Palmer's address: the middle flat in a converted Victorian house in a residential district three-quarters of a mile from the Westway estate.

They got no reply at the flat but a man in the flat below told them Palmer had gone to the races – he couldn't say which racecourse – and certainly wouldn't be back before late this evening. He might even stay overnight as he sometimes did, in which case he would probably be back around eleven tomorrow morning.

They went next to the Plough and Harrow, a picturesque pub with a pleasant atmosphere. The landlord told them Ormerod had been a regular for some years and never missed a Friday evening. If he had failed to appear that particular Friday his absence would certainly have been noticed. His pattern was always the same: he would come in at about a quarter to seven and stay until closing-time. He always sat in the same corner, rarely speaking, watching the TV or reading his paper. He would have something to eat, he would drink two half-pints during the evening, never more; he was scrupulously careful not to lose his licence. He had never been in the slightest degree troublesome. He kept very much to himself though always civil enough when spoken to. If there was any fund-raising at the pub for charity he always gave generously.

Their next call was at the council flat occupied by the Reeves, the sister and brother-in-law of Lew Dutton. They had just got back from their shopping trip, they were busy unpacking their haul of bargains. They knew nothing of what had happened and were struck dumb by what the officers had to tell them. They had neither of them ever laid eyes on Billy and had met his stepmother on only one none-too-happy occasion when they had chanced to encounter her in town with Lew one Saturday afternoon.

Once they had absorbed the dreadful news and recovered their powers of speech it was the prime concern of both of them to prevent any slur attaching, firstly and much the most importantly, to themselves, and secondly, a long way behind, to

Lew. They came across as a highly respectable couple of strong principles and inflexible views.

The officers explained that they were trying to locate Mrs Coleman to break the news to her, ask her to return home without delay. They understood she was on holiday with Lew.

The Reeves could only repeat what little Lew had told them. He had taken his remaining two weeks' holiday from work and had booked a week in a caravan; he hadn't said precisely where, merely that it was on the south coast. He had said hardly anything about the holiday. They knew he intended going with Mrs Coleman and he was well aware that they strongly disapproved of her and her way of life; her name was rarely mentioned between them. One thing he did say: if the weather proved reasonably good and if they liked the area and the caravan, they might think of staying on for the second week – there would, apparently, be no difficulty over this, out of season. The Reeves didn't know the name and address of the caravan owner nor how Lew had learned of him.

Lew hadn't sent them a postcard and they hadn't expected one. When the weather continued mild and settled they thought he would probably stay on for the second week. He didn't ring them to say so, nor had they expected him to ring. They were sure he would be back for work on Monday morning; he would probably return on Sunday evening. He would very likely drop Mrs Coleman off at her house first.

The atmosphere between the three of them had been distinctly cool since he had taken up with Mrs Coleman and they had made it plain that if he intended continuing with the relationship they would want him to move out of the flat, find somewhere else to live.

He had been staying with them for the last eight months. Before that he had been in very good digs but he had been asked to leave when his landlady needed his room – her widowed sister had decided to sell her flat in a nearby town and move in with her. The Reeves had a son, their only child, who had lived at home until he married back in the New Year. They had offered Lew the use of the vacant bedroom, believing it would be for only a month or two while he looked about, but he had settled in, the weeks had slipped into months, and he showed no sign of leaving.

'Lately, we've been expecting him to say he's decided to move in with Mrs Coleman,' Reeve volunteered but his wife flashed him a quelling glance.

'There's never been a word said about that to us,' she declared. 'I'm sure he would never have dreamed of it. She's still a married woman, not even divorced. A barmaid at a club! Done up as if she's no better than she should be. And someone else's lad thrown in with it! Not even her own son! I can't see Lew being fool enough to settle for that!'

They confirmed the description of Lew's car given by Ormerod and were able in addition to supply the registration number.

Later in the afternoon Chief Inspector Kelsey recorded appeals for both local radio and regional TV, to be broadcast in the early evening, repeated in later bulletins. The TV appeal would also go out in the south coast region, in the hope of reaching Glenna Coleman. They all included a request for any information about the present whereabouts of Billy's father.

A similar message would go out nationwide on BBC radio before the 8 a.m. and 9 a.m. news on Sunday morning.

17

The Sunday tabloids carried reports of the finding of Billy Coleman's body, ranging from a couple of paragraphs to longer and more detailed accounts, laying stress on the fact that Billy had been left alone in the house while his stepmother went off on holiday with a boyfriend.

An overwhelming response followed the Chief's appeals, with phone calls coming in until late on Saturday night and starting again with renewed force on Sunday morning. Some of the calls were from local people with something to say about the Coleman family; other callers seized the chance to air their views on the breakdown of traditional family life. There were those who had seen suspicious-looking characters in the area. Psychics, clairvoyants and mediums, many from farther afield, were eager to shed light; persons favoured with spirit visions and dream solutions were only too happy to share their revelations.

After a briefing and press conference the house-to-house teams started out once more. Officers called again at Tom Palmer's flat. It took half-a-dozen rings at his bell to bring him, sour-tempered and full of sleep, stumbling blindly to the door. He opened it a fraction and peered out in hostile silence. The officers identified themselves and asked if they might come in. He admitted them with a bad grace, he didn't ask what they wanted. He wore a dressing-gown and slippers.

In the sitting-room they told him of the discovery of Billy Coleman's body. He gawped at them with a look of horrified stupefaction. Still he said nothing but stayed slumped in his chair. They asked if he knew where Glenna Coleman could be found.

That roused him to answer: 'I'm told she went off on holiday with Lew Dutton. I don't know where.'

'You're certain she went?'

'Pretty certain. Billy told – ' He broke off, flashing them a sharp glance. He looked suddenly a good deal more wide awake.

'Billy told you she'd gone with Dutton,' one of the officers hazarded. 'He told you when you called round to the house.'

Palmer opened his mouth, plainly about to deny having called at the house, already beginning to shake his head. But before he could speak the officer added: 'Perhaps we'd better tell you we've spoken to the Colemans' neighbour, Mr Ormerod. He tells us he saw you call at the house shortly after Mrs Coleman and Dutton left, he saw your encounter with Billy.'

Palmer heard this with a deepening frown. He gave a jerky nod. 'That's right. I did call round and Billy did tell me Glenna had gone off with Dutton.'

'Did you call at the house again after that?'

He shook his head with vigour. 'No, I've never been back there since. If that's what's going on with Dutton, then I've finished with her.'

Could he tell them how he had spent the following Friday evening, 25th October, one week after Mrs Coleman and Dutton left on holiday?

90

'I can't say just like that,' he protested. 'I'd have to think about it.' He passed a hand across his jaw.

'Think about it now,' the officer pressed him. 'We're talking about a week ago this last Friday.'

'Right, yes, I've got it now.' Palmer sat up. 'That was the evening Gordon came round – Gordon's my son. He lives quite near, he's got a little flat. He came round with his mate, Tony, they work together. They're both mad on motor bikes, they want to start up a sales and repair shop, they've asked me if I'll put up some money. I told them to come round, bring all the figures, and we'd talk about it. They both came round that Friday evening.'

'Were you here with them all evening?'

'More or less. I had a drink at the pub first – the Red Lion, just around the corner. Gordon said they'd be here around half-seven, I was back here before that. They got here about a quarter to eight, they stayed till around eleven.' He supplied the addresses of both young men.

Would he have any objection if they took a look through his things?

He said nothing for some moments but shifted in his chair, finally saying: 'No, no objection. Go right ahead.'

A quick inspection of the contents of chests, cupboards and wardrobe revealed nothing that might have been the source of the grey silk threads. They then informed Palmer that they wished to take his car for forensic examination. They would keep it no longer than was absolutely necessary. Could he hand over the keys, tell them where the car was kept?

He said nothing but got to his feet with a face devoid of expression and went off to his bedroom, returning a few minutes later, dressed now in slacks and pullover, his feet clad in slip-ons. He halted on the threshold of the sitting-room, holding up the car keys.

The landlord of the Red Lion was pretty sure Palmer had been in the pub that Friday evening. He volunteered the inform-ation that to the best of his recollection Palmer had stayed only a short while, saying he was expecting his son round at the flat.

91

Gordon Palmer, unlike his father, was up, washed, shaved, dressed and breakfasted, cheerfully engaged, along with his mate Tony, in the business of the day: restoring to full working order a motor cycle they had recently bought second-hand.

Asked, without explanation, how they had spent that Friday evening, they replied immediately that they had spent it trying to persuade Gordon's father to help them get their business venture off the ground. The times they gave agreed with what Palmer had told them.

Gordon was curious to know their reason for asking but they left his curiosity unsatisfied. The breezy, carefree manner of both young men didn't suggest that they could have heard of the discovery of a boy's body in the area and the officers made no mention of it.

They did have one further question to ask: had Tom Palmer actually agreed to help finance their enterprise?

He hadn't yet decided, they were told. He had asked for a few more days to think it over, but they were very hopeful.

Towards the end of the afternoon the Chief recorded fresh appeals to go out over TV and local radio in the evening. Afterwards he sat at his desk, contemplating the progress of the investigation. The distant sporadic popping of early fireworks failed to disturb his concentration.

Dusk had fallen and the search of the Crowswood site had ended, with no significant discovery. The scrutiny of all the vehicles so far taken in had yielded not one scrap of evidence and the vehicles would now be returned.

He had before him the conclusions drawn from the analysis of both the stomach contents and the insect life found in and on the body. All tended to confirm the current estimate of the time of death: between eight and ten on the evening of Friday, 25th October.

He studied yet again the colour photographs of the three shrubs and the details supplied by the college. All three shrubs flowered freely in autumn: *Prunus subhirtella*, producing a cloud of white blossom; *Viburnum bodnantense*, a fountain-shaped shrub, with clusters of richly scented white flowers, tinged with pink; *Elaeagnus ebbingei*, with its strikingly variegated leaves, its abundance of sweetly perfumed ivory-coloured blossom.

None of the three shrubs was often seen in the average modest suburban garden. They might be looked for with more chance of success in a park or in the grounds of a public building or a larger house. If all three had been planted in close proximity it would probably be in some relatively sheltered area designed for autumn colour and scent.

So far there had been no sighting of any of the shrubs. A constable had been dispatched to make a tour of local parks, cemeteries, public gardens and displays, with no result whatever. The horticultural department of the local council had no knowledge of any of the shrubs on any of its sites. But it was still early days.

A thought pushed its way up into his brain as he laid aside the photographs: it was, of course, perfectly possible that all three sprigs had been in Billy's pocket for a day or two before 25th October. The three could have been picked from different sites on different days. They may have had nothing at all to do with his death.

He leaned back in his chair. He could see no immediately obvious motive for Billy's murder. And deliberate murder it clearly was. It wasn't brutally sadistic, there was no sex implication, no suggestion of a sudden reasonless attack by some random maniac.

The disposal of the body appeared calmly and intelligently thought out. Judging by the degree and location of the staining on the body it would seem to have been conveyed to the Crowswood site some hours after death. In the interim the body had apparently lain on its back on a hard surface, with the knees drawn up, suggesting, possibly, a confined space, such as the boot of a car.

Nothing about the death indicated any kind of gang attack by youngsters. There were no such gangs on the Westway estate, nor had the teams encountered any suggestion of youthful hostility to Billy. The killing had been swift and efficient; the disposal argued ownership – or at least access to – some kind of motor vehicle.

Sex killings, random killings, gang killings, were all mercifully

93

rare. It was family life and its stresses that appeared to account for most killings.

Shortly before eight o'clock the uniformed constable standing guard outside the Coleman house saw a car turn into the road and pull up by the gate; the registration number was that of Lew Dutton's car. As the constable spoke to the station over his radio a man and woman got out of the car and gave him frowning stares. They pushed open the gate and came swiftly up the path towards him.

'What's going on here?' the woman demanded with acrimony. 'Has that little wretch been up to something?'

Her companion placed a hand on her arm. He said nothing but directed a questioning gaze at the constable.

'Mrs Coleman?' the constable asked. 'And Mr Dutton?'

The woman gave an impatient nod. 'Yes, of course I'm Mrs Coleman! Who else? What are you doing here?'

The constable hadn't had a reply to the second part of his query. 'Mr Dutton?' he said again. The man nodded.

'I asked you what you're doing here,' the woman said with rising irritation.

'Chief Inspector Kelsey will be along in a minute or two,' the constable replied in a neutral tone. 'He'll explain everything.'

Mrs Coleman frowned even more fiercely. 'Explain what?' The constable didn't answer that but as she began to rummage in her shoulder bag for her door key he added in the same expressionless tone: 'I think it would be best if we waited out here for the Chief Inspector. He'll be here any moment.'

She made an impatient sound and whirled about to where Dutton still stood in silence. 'I'll get the cases,' Dutton said quickly and went hurrying off down the path to the car where he made it his business to drag out for as long as possible the simple procedure of opening the boot, removing the pieces of luggage, dumping them on the pavement, closing the boot again. By the time he had picked up the cases and was negotiating the gate, the Chief's car had turned the corner. Dutton set down the luggage and remained standing inside the open gate until the Chief and Sergeant Lambert had pulled up, got out and approached him. Glenna came rapidly down the path to join them.

The Chief made himself known to the pair. Glenna began firing angry questions, demanding to know what was going on, why she was being denied access to the house.

'We can go in now,' the Chief responded. 'What I've got to say is best said inside.'

That struck her dumb. She remained silent as they all went into the house. Once they were over the threshold her eyes were everywhere but there was nothing out of the way to be seen. 'Billy?' she said on a querying note. 'Where's Billy?'

Kelsey gestured them along the hall and into the living-room. 'We'll all sit down,' he said soothingly. 'Sergeant Lambert will make us some tea.'

Glenna had stopped asking questions. She sat upright in her chair, frowning slightly. She didn't look at Dutton. He reclined in his seat in an attitude of ease somewhat at variance with the expression on his face.

'I'm afraid I have bad news,' Kelsey began gently. The pair froze. 'Very bad news.' Neither met his eyes. They sat like graven images, gazing down at the carpet. 'You were asking about Billy.' As he went on to outline what had happened Glenna raised her head and stared at him with a look of incredulity. Still she said nothing. Kelsey's voice went inexorably on. When at last he fell silent she dropped her head into her hands and began to rock herself back and forth. Dutton went over and crouched by her chair. He put an arm round her shoulders. His face was creased in anxiety.

The door opened and Sergeant Lambert came in with a tray of tea. Dutton got to his feet and helped to dispense the cups. Glenna looked up at him with a dazed air. She took the cup at his urging and, again at his urging, began to drink.

Some minutes later Kelsey asked if she felt able to answer questions. She drew a long, quavering breath and closed her eyes briefly but declared herself ready.

He began by asking if she could shed any light on what had happened. Had she any idea who could possibly have done this terrible deed?

She shook her head slowly. The only person she knew of with any kind of ill feeling towards Billy was her neighbour Ormerod and she couldn't for one moment believe he could have done such a dreadful thing.

'We've had a look at Mr Ormerod,' Kelsey told her. 'We've no reason at this moment to suppose he had anything to do with it.'

Glenna embarked, nevertheless, on a long-winded account of the episode of Ormerod's dog. Kelsey broke in to tell her they were aware of all that, they were definitely not at present interested in Ormerod. He went on to ask if she could tell them the name of any special friends of Billy's; they already knew of David Willcox. Again she shook her head. She knew nothing of any friends he might have had, at school or on the estate; she had known nothing of David Willcox. 'Billy never brought any friend home?' Kelsey queried. Once more she shook her head, without speaking.

He raised the question of the money found in the box under Billy's bed. Did she know how he had come by it?

She moved her shoulders. 'Could be from running errands or doing odd jobs, washing cars, maybe. I couldn't really say.' She had known nothing of the money, she was surprised to hear of the amount. 'I never poked my nose into his business.' She gave the Chief a forthright glance. 'He was no responsibility of mine. I was talking to a customer at the club – he works for a solicitor. He told me step-parents don't have any legal responsibilities – or any legal rights, for that matter.'

Her words began to tumble out. 'I haven't had any money from Billy's father for long enough. I've never heard a word from him, I've no idea where he is. Billy was always so sure his Dad would come back, he tried to kid himself his Dad loved him but there wasn't much evidence of that that I could see. He never wrote Billy a line, never sent him a card or a present at Christmas or on his birthday, never picked up a phone to speak to him.' She fell abruptly silent.

The Chief brought up the name of Tom Palmer. She confirmed that she had broken off with him because of his drinking, his bouts of aggressive behaviour. But she couldn't believe he would ever lay a finger on the boy. When Kelsey went on to speak of Palmer's call at the house, the way he had lashed out at Billy, she expressed surprise.

Kelsey pressed her on the point. Was it not conceivable that in a later call Palmer could have struck out more savagely, particularly if he had been in drink, fired by anger at her association with Dutton? She conceded, reluctantly, that it was a possibility.

Had she gone off before, leaving Billy on his own?

She answered without hesitation. She had gone off twice before, for a long weekend on both occasions. 'Billy got along fine both times,' she declared. 'He didn't mind me going, he quite enjoyed being on his own. He was an independent kid, sharp as a monkey, sensible in lots of ways, careful with lights, fires, locking up properly, all that kind of thing. I always left him enough money, he was good with money, didn't go wasting it on rubbish.' She fixed Kelsey with her eye. 'I could have managed fine by myself at that age. I'd have thought I was in paradise, having the house to myself, enough money, TV, able to please myself what I did, where I went, no one to answer to.'

No, she hadn't asked anyone to keep an eye on Billy while she was away. 'He'd have hated that,' she stated with certainty. 'I'd have hated it myself, at his age. I more or less brought myself up and it did me no harm. It's a hard old world, you've got to look out for yourself, you might as well learn early on.'

Dutton had listened to all this without uttering a word. Kelsey asked him now at what point they had decided to stay on in the caravan for another week.

His manner was quiet and straightforward as he answered. He looked directly at the Chief, he never glanced at Glenna.

It was Glenna who had brought up the subject one evening, suggesting they might stay on. He had agreed. Glenna had then rung Billy. Billy didn't mind in the least and said he still had plenty of money left. Dutton rang the caravan owner next day and arranged matters.

When exactly had these two phone calls taken place?

In the slight pause that followed, Dutton slid a glance at Glenna. She immediately spoke up. 'I rang Billy on the Wednesday evening and Lew rang the owner on the Thursday morning.' Dutton nodded several times. 'I told Billy to be sure to get himself off to school on time on Monday morning,' she went on. 'He said he would. I had no worries about that. He was always up early, always got himself ready in good time.'

When Kelsey went on to ask for the name, address and phone number of the caravan owner there was another, lengthier pause and then, after some searching through his pockets, Dutton finally produced the information, still without speaking. The pair of them were now looking very subdued.

Kelsey said they would need to take a look through the cases the pair had brought back from holiday. They would also be taking Dutton's car in for examination, they would keep it no longer than necessary. Kelsey had already explained to Glenna that they had looked through her things and had examined her car, in the course of routine investigation. She had accepted all that without any show of resentment. Dutton, therefore, could scarcely have been surprised that his own vehicle was to receive similar treatment. But he began at once to voice a strong protest and then suddenly fell silent, contenting himself with saying, a minute or two later: 'It's going to be very inconvenient.'

'You can stop on here,' Glenna instantly offered. 'I can run you to work in the morning, pick you up again in the evening.'

He didn't meet her eye. 'I'd better not,' he said heavily after some moments. 'I'd better get back to the flat.'

The inspection of the holiday cases revealed nothing of significance. There were still questions to be answered. How had they spent the evening of Friday, 25th October?

They replied readily. They had spent the evening in a pub, from around seven thirty until closing-time, with two other couples also on holiday in the area. They had come across the couples at a theme park a day or two before and it had been arranged that they should all meet on the Friday evening. The other two couples were not previously known to each other but were staying in the same hotel. Both couples had come to the end of their holiday and were returning home on the Saturday morning.

After leaving the pub Dutton and Glenna had driven back to the caravan and gone straight to bed.

They had bought no newspapers, they had known nothing of the TV and radio appeals. Their car had been parked beside the caravan, which stood with two others in a large field. Neither of the other two caravans had been occupied during that fortnight.

Yes, they could give the names of the couples they had spent the evening with. They didn't know their home addresses but they did know the name of the hotel where they had been staying.

When Kelsey asked Glenna if she was ready to go with them to the mortuary to make the formal identification she closed her eyes and sat silent for some moments, then she opened her eyes, squared her shoulders and told him she was ready. Dutton had made no kind of response and she sent him a beseeching glance. Still he remained silent and motionless.

'You'll come with me?' she said at last on a rising note. She looked on the verge of tears. There was a moment's silence. He didn't meet her eye.

'*Please!*' she begged.

He gave a reluctant nod, he still didn't look at her. When they stood up to go he didn't take her arm but walked out to the police car a few paces behind her, still in silence.

In the car, Glenna leaned back against the upholstery with her eyes closed. She stumbled slightly as she left the car but Dutton didn't put out a hand to steady her. She walked with faltering steps and lowered head until the inescapable moment when she had to look down at Billy. She began to weep, little shuddering sobs, her face contorted in an effort at control. Dutton stood to one side, silent and unmoving, never once so much as glancing at the body.

Outside in the corridor again, Glenna leaned against the wall, dabbing at her eyes. During the drive back to the house none of the four spoke a word.

18

It was plain on Monday morning that interest in the case on the part of the tabloid press showed no sign of diminishing.

Instructions were issued to the house-to-house teams to inquire for any sightings of Dutton's car, or of Dutton or Glenna in person, in the area during Friday, 25th October.

An attempt was made to contact the owner of the caravan rented by Dutton but the owner was out on business and couldn't be reached until after lunch.

When the Chief visited Billy's school his eye was taken by the vast array of bunches of flowers bordering the approaches and perimeter. The children and staff were assembled in the hall. The headmaster introduced the Chief and the two women detective constables accompanying him. The Chief addressed

99

the assembly in as quiet and undramatic a fashion as possible, asking for any information, any sightings of Billy that Friday. When the Chief left the school the two women officers stayed behind to chat at greater length and more informally to the children after they had returned to their classrooms.

The officers reported on getting back to the station that a boy in the class below Billy's had come forward to say he had seen Billy at around eight forty-five that Friday evening, about a quarter of a mile from the Westway estate, walking away from the estate. He hadn't spoken to Billy and Billy hadn't seen him; they were on opposite sides of the road. He was asked if he could be sure it was Billy, glimpsed yards away under street lighting, but he maintained stubbornly that he was in no doubt. It was put to him that it might have been some previous evening he was remembering but he shook his head vigorously. It was definitely that Friday, though he couldn't explain why he was so certain.

A discreet word with the boy's class teacher revealed that the boy couldn't be considered a totally reliable source of information; he was always one to seek the limelight and furthermore could easily persuade himself of the reality of what it suited him to believe.

When the caravan owner was finally contacted after lunch he had a different tale to tell about Dutton's booking of the extra week. Yes, Dutton had certainly mentioned, when the original booking was made, that he might be interested in an additional week. Dutton was told that would be no problem, he should just give a ring if he decided to stay on.

In the event Dutton had phoned about noon on the Saturday to say he wanted the extra week. Yes, the owner was quite sure it was the Saturday. Not having heard anything, he had concluded Dutton had abandoned the idea and had been surprised to hear from him. He had noted the date as he always did in his record of bookings, which he consulted at the police request. Yes, the record confirmed what he had just told them: Dutton had rung around noon on the Saturday, 26th October. His cheque had arrived in the post on the Monday morning.

In the early afternoon Sergeant Lambert drove the Chief round

100

to the Westway estate. They saw that not a single flower had been laid before the Coleman house. Glenna was sitting watching TV when Lambert rang her doorbell. She didn't wait to be told why they had called but began, the moment she opened the door, a vociferous complaint about the way she was being treated on the estate. She had gone to the corner shop for a few items and the woman had refused to serve her. She had been told very plainly that her custom was no longer wanted. Other customers in the shop had made it equally clear that they shared these views.

She had returned home, got into her car and driven into town, finding a shop where she wasn't known, to make her purchases. As she drove back on to the estate she had been the target of abusive shouts from a group of youths.

'And that's not all of it!' she declared vehemently. She had phoned her boss first thing this morning to say she wouldn't be in at all today. He had rung back later in the morning and to all intents and purposes sacked her. 'He said the other staff won't have me working there and the customers wouldn't have me serving in the bar. He said he couldn't argue with that. He'll speak to his accountant, he'll be in touch with me again when they decide what he's going to pay me.' She looked about to burst into tears. 'I've only worked there for eighteen months so I've no comeback. I've no chance of getting another job round here.'

'I think you should consider leaving Westway,' Kelsey advised. 'For the time being, at any rate.' He knew from the teams how strongly feeling was running against her on the estate. He had come with the intention of advising her to leave, before hearing what she had to say.

She set her jaw. 'I'll do no such thing! I won't be driven out of the house! In any case, where would I go?'

'Is there no friend you could go to? Someone not too far away, where we can get in touch with you if need be?' She gave a shake of her head.

'I'm sure we could find you somewhere,' Kelsey offered but again she shook her head. 'I should think it over if I were you,' he persisted. 'If you do change your mind or if there's any trouble, give us a ring.'

She gave a brief nod. 'I'll be all right,' she assured him. 'You've no need to worry about me.'

Kelsey had a news briefing coming up shortly and he had also arranged to make further TV and radio appeals later in the afternoon. Now he invited Glenna to take part with him in all these, make her voice heard. But she was adamant in her refusal. 'I'd be far too nervous,' she maintained. 'I wouldn't know what to say. And it wouldn't do me any good here on the estate. They'd be against me more than ever.' He saw she wasn't to be persuaded.

'Is that what you came here to ask me?' she inquired.

'That, and something else,' he told her. 'This business of exactly when Lew Dutton booked the extra week. You both told us it was on the Thursday morning. We now know for certain it was on the Saturday morning.'

She bit her lip. 'Yes, it was the Saturday,' she conceded at last. 'I could see the way your mind was working, I was terrified of what you might be thinking.' She gazed earnestly up at him. 'It wasn't all lies. I did ring Billy on the Wednesday evening after we'd talked about staying on. Lew did try to ring the owner on the Thursday morning but he couldn't get him. He tried again on the Friday but he had no luck. He finally got him on the Saturday morning.' She clasped her hands tightly. 'Lew did try his best to be friendly to Billy.'

'How did Billy respond?' Kelsey asked.

There was a brief silence, then she said: 'All right,' in a flat voice. 'I'm positive he'd have got round to accepting Lew in the end.'

At five thirty Kelsey drove over to the Reeves' flat. Sergeant Lambert followed, driving Dutton's car, which had now been cleared.

Neither Reeve nor Dutton had yet arrived home from work but Mrs Reeve had just got in from her job at a day-care centre. When Kelsey introduced himself her manner was far from welcoming but she allowed them to come in and wait for Dutton, whom she expected shortly. Her face was set and hostile as she took them along to the living-room. She was about to depart to the kitchen quarters when she halted in the doorway as if forced to give voice to her thoughts: 'I see that Glenna Coleman hasn't dared show her face on TV. It's my belief she knows a lot more about that boy's death than she's letting on.' Her face was alight with venom.

Kelsey gazed calmly back at her. 'She assures us she was with your brother all the way along, from 18th October, right through to getting back to Westway last night. Is it your belief that your brother also knows more about Billy's death than he's letting on?'

That brought her up sharp. Her expression changed instantly to one of marked wariness. As she opened her mouth to respond there came the sound of the front door opening and closing, footsteps in the hall. 'That'll be Lew now!' She wheeled round to leave the room but Dutton entered before she reached the threshold. He didn't appear surprised, he had seen the two cars outside.

'I see I've got my car back,' he said to Kelsey by way of greeting. His manner was composed and businesslike. Lambert handed him the car keys.

The Chief came straight to the point. He told Dutton he now knew for certain the extra week had been booked on the Saturday morning. Why had Dutton maintained it was two days earlier?

Dutton didn't lose his unruffled air. 'I'd have told you it was on the Saturday, I'd no reason to say anything else. But when Glenna spoke up and said it was on the Thursday, what else could I do but go along with her? I didn't know why she'd said what she did but I could hardly call her a liar to her face.'

'Do you know now why she said what she did?' Kelsey asked.

He shook his head. 'I haven't spoken to her since I left the house last night.' He didn't inquire how she was bearing up, he expressed not the slightest concern. 'It occurred to me pretty well right away that you'd get on to the owner, you'd discover the truth about the booking, so I couldn't see that any great harm had been done.'

'Can you make any guess now as to why Glenna said what she did?'

He shrugged. 'I gave up a long time ago trying to guess what women mean by what they say.'

Kelsey switched tack. 'How did you get on with Billy?'

He pulled down the corners of his mouth. 'Well enough. I tried to be friendly but it was slow going. I didn't expect him to be all

103

over me, I could see he missed his Dad. He was never rude or cheeky. I was pretty sure we'd get on all right, given time.'

'Was it on the cards you'd be moving in with Glenna?'

Again he shrugged. 'It was mentioned once or twice. Nothing definite. There was no great rush.'

Before they left they made a quick, fruitless inspection of Dutton's things.

One of the women officers who had talked to the schoolchildren went along at nine on Tuesday morning to speak to Billy's friend, David Willcox. David's father had taken time off work.

David was still in bed. He was as small and slight as Billy and though still pale seemed well on the way to recovery.

He was greatly intrigued by the arrival of a policewoman, although he had no idea why she should wish to speak to him. In the presence of both parents, gently and sympathetically, she broke the news of Billy's death.

David was incredulous, shocked and horrified, he wept broken-heartedly. When at last he was comparatively calm he showed no reluctance to answer questions. As Billy's best friend he plainly felt it his clear duty to help the investigation in any way he could.

During the questioning his parents sat behind the bed where David couldn't see them. They had agreed on no account to interrupt or make any kind of comment.

The constable began by asking if Billy had ever mentioned Lew Dutton to him.

David answered in uncertain tones at first, still deeply upset, but after a few minutes his voice grew steadier. Yes, Billy had mentioned Dutton several times. Billy didn't like Dutton, not because Dutton had been in any way unkind to him but because he was sure his stepmother would like Dutton to move into the house and Billy couldn't tolerate the notion of another man taking his father's place.

Billy had actively disliked Tom Palmer who had never made any effort to get on with him but he never gave any thought to Palmer in recent times as he was certain his stepmother had lost interest in him.

When the constable spoke of the money found in the box

104

under Billy's bed, David showed no surprise but looked ill at ease. 'I think you may be able to tell us where he got the money from,' the constable suggested gently. 'It may be that you don't like telling, you may feel you're being disloyal to your friend, giving away his secrets. I can understand that, but knowing about the money might help us to find out who killed Billy. And whatever you tell us can't hurt Billy now.'

David digested this in silence. 'I do know where he got the money,' he said at last. There was another silence before he went on. He looked at the constable as he spoke. Tears glittered in his eyes. 'He was saving up so he could run away and try to find his father.' He paused again, closed his eyes briefly, then continued in a voice stripped of all expression: 'He stole things from houses.' His mother jerked up in her seat. The constable flashed her a warning glance and she subsided.

David went on: 'He sold the things to a man on the estate, he goes to car boot sales, he buys and sells things. Billy only ever stole little things and he only took one or two at a time. He never took things from shops, only houses. He picked houses where it looked as if the people had plenty of money. He used to walk around in the evenings, looking for houses where it would be easy to get in and out again. He never broke a window or anything like that. And he never tried to get into a house where there was a dog, or children. He used to walk about most evenings but he only stole something about once a week or once a fortnight. He said he was sure some people never knew anyone had been in and taken something, they never missed what he'd stolen...' His voice tailed off into silence.

'Do you know the name of the man who bought the things from Billy?' the constable asked.

He nodded. 'Mr Shardlow. He works at Paragon. Billy said he never gave him much for the things. He tried to get him to pay more but Mr Shardlow wouldn't. Billy didn't know anyone else he could sell them to.'

'Do you know if there are any other children who steal things and then sell them to Mr Shardlow?'

No, David didn't know of anyone else.

She asked if Billy had been on good terms with Mr Shardlow.

'No, not really,' David replied without hesitation. 'He thought Mr Shardlow was cheating him. He used to look in the windows

105

of antique shops and if he saw something that looked like something he'd stolen he'd go in and ask how much it was. He said it was always a terrific lot more than he'd ever got from Mr Shardlow.' He fell silent, looking down with an uncomfortable air. Then he continued, awkwardly. 'He said he told Mr Shardlow he'd shop him to the police if he didn't give him more for the things and Mr Shardlow said if he did that the police would get Billy as well.'

Did he know if Mr Shardlow had ever struck Billy?

David met her eyes again. 'He tried to sometimes but Billy always managed to dodge him.'

The inquest on William Edward Coleman was set down for 11 a.m. The formal proceedings took little time, the inquest being opened and adjourned without any date being set for resumption. The body was released for burial.

Afterwards, Sergeant Lambert drove the Chief over to Westway to have a word with Matthew Shardlow. They found him at home, cleaning his windows. The Chief introduced himself and asked if they might go indoors for a word. He agreed readily. It was plain that he recognized the Chief from his appearances on TV. 'A dreadful business about poor Billy Coleman,' he observed as he took them into the living-room.

'It's about Billy we'd like to talk to you,' Kelsey said.

Shardlow appeared in no way perturbed. He looked with alert interest at the Chief, waiting for him to go on.

'I gather you knew the boy,' Kelsey said.

'Indeed I did,' Shardlow responded at once. 'He wasn't a bad kid.'

Kelsey regarded him. 'I'm given to understand he was in the habit of entering houses and stealing small ornaments which he then sold to you.'

Shardlow's face expressed wounded astonishment. 'Who on earth told you that? I certainly bought little odds and ends from him, things of no value. He said they'd come to him from his mother – she died a few years back, she was a nice, quiet woman. Billy knew I go to car boot sales. He came round one day, back in the New Year, it would be, he wanted to know if I'd give him a few bob for a little flower vase he had, the sort of

106

thing you might win at a fair. I said sure, I didn't want to disappoint the kid. I put it in with my other stuff for the next car boot sale. Billy came back four or five times after that with little pieces, I can't remember now what they were but they were none of them worth more than a few bob.' He gave a faint smile. 'I'm afraid someone's been pulling your leg, Chief Inspector, trying to make out poor Billy was a housebreaker.'

'These things you sell at the car boot sales,' Kelsey said. 'How do you come by them?'

Again a ready response. 'I buy job lots at the auction rooms. I used to work there years ago, I know the form. There's always a box or two of jumble at the tail end of a sale, they go for next to nothing. You never know what you're going to find when you sort through them. I've had one or two nice little pieces out of those boxes in my time. If I come across something really good – which doesn't happen very often – then I take it into one of the antique shops in town, they all know me. The rest of the stuff I sell at the car boot sales.' He grinned. 'Once in a while I get lucky there as well, I spot something good among the stuff the other carbooters are flogging. I pass it on to a dealer or take it into an antique shop.' He moved his head. 'It's a nice little hobby, plenty of interest. You get some real characters among the carbooters. Some of them make quite a decent living out of it.'

'Were you always on good terms with Billy?' Kelsey inquired.

Shardlow looked surprised. 'Yes, of course I was. Why wouldn't I be?'

'Did you never have an argument over money?'

He gave a quick shake of his head. 'No, never. He was always more than satisfied.'

'Did you never lose your temper? Lash out at him?'

Shardlow frowned. 'Look here,' he responded on a note of strong protest, 'I don't know who you've been talking to and I don't know what you're getting at, but I'm telling you there was never anything like that. We were always on the best of terms. Just ask yourself this: would Billy have come here half-a-dozen times if I'd treated him the way you're trying to suggest?'

Kelsey studied him in silence, then he invited Shardlow to cast his mind back to Friday, 25th October. Could he say how he had spent that evening?

'No trouble,' Shardlow replied at once. 'I went round to my

mother's. I always go round there on a Friday evening. I go round other evenings as well, depending on how things work out, but I always go without fail on a Friday, it's been like that for years. You can ask her yourself, she'll tell you. She's turned seventy now, she gets a bit of trouble with arthritis. I keep her garden tidy for her, I do any little jobs that want doing round the house, then I spend a bit of time in the workshop. My Dad set that up. I took it on after he died, I kept it on after I got married.'

Again Kelsey studied him in silence. Shardlow sat untroubled by his gaze. When Kelsey told him they'd like to take a look through his things he made no objection. He followed them about, standing in the doorway of whatever room was engaging their attention. When it was finished, having yielded nothing, Kelsey asked what vehicle Shardlow drove. He was told it was an estate car, a few years old, very useful for ferrying stuff about. Kelsey told him they'd like to take it, look it over, they would return it as soon as possible.

Shardlow showed no surprise, uttered no word of complaint. 'I'll get the keys,' he responded at once. 'The car's out in the garage.'

As soon as Kelsey got back to the station he sent a constable along to the auction rooms where Shardlow had worked. A porter there confirmed what Shardlow had told them about his buying of job lots. He also often bought damaged or dilapidated pieces of old furniture to restore and sell on. 'It's just a hobby with him,' the porter added, 'but he's pretty good at that sort of thing.'

The constable went from the auction room to the cottage owned by Shardlow's mother. Yes, she told him, Matthew came round every Friday evening, he hadn't missed one for a very long time, except, of course, when he was away on holiday. He usually arrived at around six thirty and stayed until around ten fifteen. She couldn't precisely recall that particular Friday but she would certainly remember if he had arrived later or left earlier than usual. A man to be relied on, her son Matthew. 'No mother ever had a better son,' she declared with total conviction.

When the constable asked, without offering any explanation, if he might look through her things, she was greatly puzzled but she didn't refuse permission. Once again, the search yielded nothing.

Immediately after lunch DC Slade was dispatched to the south coast. He was able to locate without difficulty the caravan Dutton had rented. It stood, as Dutton had said, with two others in a large field; the farmer confirmed that neither of the other two had been occupied since the end of September.

Slade went on to the hotel where the two couples named by Dutton had stayed. Yes, he was told, both couples had stayed there; both had left at the end of their holiday, after breakfast on the Saturday morning, 26th October. Slade was given both home addresses: one in a town some sixty miles to the north, the other further north still, another thirty miles on.

He set off at once on his first call and was lucky enough to find both husband and wife in.

They were not entirely surprised to receive a visit from the Cannonbridge police. In the days following their return from holiday they had become aware of the Billy Coleman murder, had occasionally seen newspaper and TV coverage. They had gradually realized with astonishment and revulsion that the Mrs Glenna Coleman they had spent an evening with was the step-mother of the murdered boy, abandoned by her to his own devices while she went jaunting off with her boyfriend. It was abundantly plain that they now felt strong animosity towards both Glenna and Dutton and equally plain, when Slade asked them for an account of that Friday evening, that it would only be with the greatest reluctance that they would be able to bring themselves to put the pair in the clear. They wanted nothing at all to do with the case. They both felt, moreover, that they were being in some way used by the pair to avert suspicion.

Slade wasn't surprised, therefore, when his questions were at first met with a not-at-all-sure, don't-quite-recall type of response. But he persisted, courteously and doggedly. In the end the best he could get was an acknowledgement that they had met the pair for drinks one evening. But they couldn't by any means be persuaded to say with certainty which evening that was. Yes, it could have been the Friday but it could equally well have been the Thursday.

Had either Glenna or Dutton said exactly when they intended returning home? Had either of them mentioned staying on at the caravan for another week?

They thought about this, they made low-voiced exchanges before finally agreeing on a reply: while nothing specific had been said, they both had the impression that the holiday had been for one week only and that the pair would be returning home next day. Neither could remember anything being said about staying on for an extra week.

Slade looked at his watch as he got back into his car. A quick snack and then the road north again. Find himself a bed for the night when he reached his destination, then up first thing in the morning to catch the second couple before they could leave for work.

By 6.30 p.m. the bonfires were crackling fiercely on the Westway estate. In back gardens, in the light of leaping flames, the family parties baked their potatoes, ooh-ing and aah-ing at the showers of golden rain, the multi-coloured explosions, brilliant set pieces.

Glenna Coleman hadn't stirred from the house all day, not even as far as the garden. No one had been near her. She could have driven into town to do a little shopping but she was afraid she might return to find her windows smashed, her walls daubed with paint.

Her phone had rung a good many times, always with anonymous, abusive calls. She daren't leave the phone off the hook or let it ring unanswered in case it should be the police trying to get in touch with her. Her current tactics were to snatch up the receiver at the first ring, slam it back down the instant she identified it as a nuisance call.

She had spent the day cleaning, tidying, washing, for something to do. She had shampooed her hair, done her nails. She had sat in front of the TV – she could scarcely be said to have watched it as she couldn't keep her attention focused on the programmes, but she kept the TV on all the same; the faces and voices gave her an illusion of company. The thought of tomorrow horrified her: what could she possibly find to fill the endless hours?

When it grew dark she drew the curtains but daren't put any lights on. At least she had the illumination from the TV to pierce the gloom. Outside, she could hear the bangs, the swooshes and whistles. The evening dragged interminably by. She grew hungry and thirsty. She felt her way into the kitchen, found something to eat, a can of soft drink. She took them back to the living-room, ate and drank in the shadowy darkness. She leaned back into the sofa, closed her eyes and felt herself mercifully beginning to drift off to sleep.

She was suddenly jerked wide awake by the sound of voices outside. Right outside the house. Her heart began to thump. The voices grew louder, more careless; there was laughter, boo-ing, jeers and taunts. She got to her feet and crept to the window, she drew the end of a curtain a little way aside and peered out.

By the gate was a gang of youths, fifteen or twenty of them, armed with flaming branches. She stood for an instant frozen in terror but then roused herself. She must do something and do it now, she couldn't let them burn the house down with herself inside it. The police – she must ring the police. As she was about to turn from the window she saw, to her overwhelming joy and relief, a police patrol car pull up outside. She remained where she was, watching.

The youngsters didn't take to their heels but stayed put, arguing with the two policemen, waving their flaming branches, gesticulating towards the house. The policemen raised their hands, palm outwards, in a quieting fashion. They began to edge the youths away from the house. One of them spoke into his radio.

She stayed by the window, following every movement. When a second patrol car arrived, a brief consultation took place between all four officers, then one of them opened her gate and came up the path. She left the window, switched on a light and darted out into the passage. She snatched open the front door as the first sharp ring sounded on the bell.

The officer didn't come in. He didn't have to spend time trying to persuade her to leave, she was already fully persuaded. 'Give me five minutes,' she said. She ran to the phone, tapped out the number of the Reeves' flat. She closed her eyes in a moment's relief when Lew Dutton answered. She poured out a swift ex-planation, throwing herself on his mercy. Could he come over right away and get her? As soon as they were off the estate they could decide where she was to go.

111

But Lew was sorry, he couldn't help. He felt it best all round if he kept out of this. He said no more but replaced the receiver.

She stood in shock for no more than an instant. She tapped out another number, that of the club, she asked urgently to speak to Mrs Quirke. When Edna came to the phone Glenna again poured out an explanation. This time she got a very different response.

'I'll leave my house keys with the doorman,' Edna said at once. She gave the address of her cottage – Glenna had never been out there. 'Make yourself at home,' she urged. 'Get yourself anything you like to eat or drink. I'll be home around twelve thirty.'

Glenna threw some things into a bag. She ran round, switching off and securing, and then left the house, locking it behind her.

The four policemen were still by the gate. The air reverberated with thuds and explosions but there was no sign now of the youths with their flaming torches.

She was still shaking as she drove her little car out of the garage, down into the road. She got out of the car and handed over her house keys to an officer, for return to the council. 'I'll never set foot on this estate again!' she vowed fiercely. She got into the rear of the car while an officer took the driver's seat; his colleague would follow in the patrol car. The other patrol car would remain on the estate to make sure there was no further trouble.

She lay down on the rear seat, out of sight, until they were off the estate. They took the road, first to the club and then out to Edna's cottage. When she was safely installed the two policemen drove off in their patrol car.

Alone in the cottage, Glenna walked restlessly about, upstairs and down. She made herself coffee, nibbled at a biscuit, before dropping on to the living-room sofa, all at once totally exhausted. She leaned back and closed her eyes.

It struck her with sudden shattering force that she had lost her house, lost it for good. She began to weep, her shoulders shaking with great racking sobs.

The lingering smell of bonfires and fireworks hung over the Westway estate next morning as council workmen removed

Glenna's belongings before boarding up the premises. The house wouldn't be relet until things had calmed down. Glenna's possessions would be taken to a council storage depot where she would have access to them until she was able to decide on long-term plans. The police had let it be widely known on the estate that Glenna had left and would under no circumstances ever return. They would keep an eye on the house but expected no further trouble.

Miles away to the north, DC Slade had risen early. Shortly before eight he arrived on the doorstep of the second couple named by Dutton. They received him in a much more friendly and helpful fashion. Yes, they could spare the time to talk to him now; neither had to be at work before nine.

Yes, they had read about the case and had seen the coverage on TV. And yes, they had come to realize that the dead boy was the stepson of the Mrs Coleman they had met on holiday. They had liked both Glenna and Dutton and were not as ready as the first couple to be censorious and judgemental.

They had no difficulty in recalling the events of that Friday evening. They were certain it was on the Friday when all six of them had met for a drink at around seven thirty; they had made a point of doing most of their packing before setting off for the pub as they wanted to be sure of an early start next morning. All six of them had stayed in the pub until closing-time.

They both clearly recalled someone asking Dutton in the course of conversation if, like the other four, he and Mrs Coleman would be off home in the morning. Dutton had launched into an account of how the two of them had decided they would like to stay on for another week. They had tried without success to contact the owner of the caravan they were renting but they were confident of reaching him next morning.

Could either of them remember if anything had been said that could shed light on exactly when the pair had decided they would like to stay on?

They both pondered in silence, without consulting each other. At last the wife spoke up. She could recall Mrs Coleman saying they had talked it over and made their decision two days earlier – the Wednesday, that would be. They had been tempted to stay on largely because Wednesday had been an exceptionally mild and beautiful day. Yes, she was certain Mrs Coleman had said this, and yes, she was also certain that the Wednesday had indeed been a particularly lovely day.

Chief Inspector Kelsey had arranged another TV appearance for Wednesday evening, to be recorded during the afternoon. He sent a woman constable out to Edna Quirke's cottage to talk to Glenna, in the hope that a female officer might have more success in persuading her to take part in the recording. But the constable had no better luck. Glenna was adamant she would not appear, now or on any future occasion; it was a waste of time trying to talk her into it. 'The next thing would be I'd have the folk round here getting together to drive me out,' she maintained fiercely. 'I've had enough of that. And I'm positive Edna wouldn't thank me for it. I'm lying low here and I intend to keep on lying low.'

When DC Slade got back to Cannonbridge, Kelsey listened with close attention to what he had to say, then he got Slade to go through again every detail of his interview with the second couple.

In the late afternoon there was a return of material from the forensic laboratory, among it the small folded square of decorative gold-coloured foil from Billy's pocket; this was, it seemed, a confectionery wrapper. Kelsey handed it to an officer with instructions to set about tracing its origins first thing next morning.

At the end of the day Kelsey sat at his desk in a mood of some despondency as he reviewed the state of the investigation. All their efforts had failed to locate Billy's father. There had been no results of any value from the posters, the questioning of motorists in the Crowswood area. The house-to-house teams had uncovered no sightings of Dutton's car or of either Dutton or Glenna, anywhere in the vicinity of Westway during the nine days immediately following their departure for the south coast. Shardlow's car had now been cleared and returned to him. They were no nearer discovering the source of the grey silk threads.

They hadn't come across a single specimen of any of the three shrubs.

He felt worn out, irritated, frustrated; he had the beginnings of a headache. Time to break off for the night, go home, get some rest.

As he pushed back his chair and stood up he remembered that the inquest on Robert Anstey was due to be resumed on Friday morning. How long ago now it seemed since he had been devoting his time to that case. He wondered how Lilian Anstey was bearing up, if she had regained her equilibrium. Better call in on her tomorrow morning on his way to work, catch her before she set off for Paragon. See how she was faring, offer a word of support, assure her everything was all set for Friday. The inquest would in all likelihood be concluded; she would very probably find it a good deal less of an ordeal than she feared.

He slept long and heavily. He was still fuzzy-headed from fatigue when the alarm woke him. It was a good ten minutes before he was able to force himself out of bed, resisting all the while the insidious temptation to turn over, sink back into the trough of sleep.

Once he was up, everything conspired to delay him further. He was by no means in the sunniest of tempers when at length he closed the door of his flat and went across to the garage. He looked at his watch as he got into his car. He might just about manage to catch Lilian.

By the time he reached Kincraig his mood had lifted somewhat. It was a dry, bright morning, mild for early November. His fatigue was ebbing, he began to feel almost lively as he turned in through the gates.

He rang the front doorbell once, twice, three times, without answer. No sound from within. Lilian must have left for work. Mrs Whiting might not yet have arrived. As he turned from the door he heard steps somewhere at the rear of the house. He went round and saw Mrs Whiting a few yards away, coming up from the garden. She gave him a wave of acknowledgement. 'I won't be a moment,' she called. 'Take your time,' he called back. 'No rush.' She had been carrying faded flowers down to the compost heap, she stopped now to pick up some she had dropped on the path. She returned to the compost heap with them and then set off again for the house.

Kelsey stood looking idly about him. A spectacular sumach tree caught his eye, the slender leaves fringed in scarlet and green. A drift of scent reached his nostrils. He half turned in its direction and halted abruptly, the hair prickling along his scalp.

He was looking at an area planted with shrubs, a sheltered, curving bay, where someone standing concealed, observing comings and goings, waiting a chance to dart in through the back door, might take a moment to pluck a sprig of scented blossom, drop it into a pocket.

The shrubs were still in flowering splendour. The three in the front of the bay Kelsey knew so well, had scrutinized so often, so minutely, in their colour reproductions. He could have recited their names in his sleep: *Prunus subhirtella, Viburnum bodnantense, Elaeagnus ebbingei.*

19

Kelsey stood motionless. The schoolboy in the lower class had been positive he had spotted Billy at around eight forty-five that Friday evening. Billy's feet, from what the boy had said, could have been taking him in this direction.

Mrs Whiting came hurrying up to where he stood. 'If you were wanting a word with Mrs Anstey,' she said, 'I'm afraid you've missed her. She goes early these days.'

'I'll look in again this evening,' Kelsey told her. 'I'd rather you didn't mention to her that I called. I wouldn't want her worrying unnecessarily. It's only a word about tomorrow, the resumed inquest.'

She gave a nod of acquiescence. 'I've seen you on TV a few times lately,' she remarked as she walked with him round to the front of the house. 'What a dreadful case that is, that poor Coleman boy. You must have your hands full with that.'

In the middle of the afternoon Kelsey had a report from the officer seeking the origins of the foil. He had made a round of wholesale and retail confectioners in the area and the foil had now definitely been identified as the wrapper used for an expensive brand of marrons glacés.

When Kelsey returned to Kincraig shortly after six Hester Whiting said in a low voice as she admitted him: 'I haven't said anything about you being here this morning.'

Lilian had got in from Paragon some fifteen minutes earlier. She looked a good deal less tired and strained, more composed.

As Hester was about to go back to the kitchen Kelsey said: 'Don't go. I'd like you to see this, too.' He produced the square of foil, fully opened out now in its cellophane envelope, the distinctive pattern clearly visible. He held it out, asked if it meant anything to either of them.

They were both silent for a moment or two, gazing down at it. 'It looks like the foil on those sweets Mrs Farrell brought,' Hester said at last. 'Those French chestnut things.'

'I believe you're right!' Lilian struck in. 'Marrons glacés,' she added to Kelsey. 'Bridget brought me some a week or two back.'

'When was that?' Kelsey asked.

'It was –' Lilian began, breaking off suddenly with a look of distress. 'It was the evening –' She broke off again.

Hester came to her rescue. 'It was that Friday evening,' she said to Kelsey with a significant look. 'Mrs Farrell called in just before Mrs Anstey went to the dinner with Mr and Mrs Joslin.'

'Neither of you mentioned these sweets earlier,' Kelsey said.

They both looked surprised. 'I never gave them a second thought,' Lilian said.

'Neither did I,' Hester put in. 'With all that happened, I never thought of them again.' She added with a puzzled air: 'I don't know that I'd have mentioned the sweets if I had remembered them. I wouldn't have seen any reason to mention them.'

'I don't think I would, either,' Lilian said. 'I'm sure Robert didn't eat any, if that's what you're thinking. He hardly ever ate sweets or chocolates and he never liked the taste of chestnuts.'

Kelsey asked where the rest of the marrons were now.

After a little thought the two women decided that the box had probably been put in the chiffonier standing against the sitting-room wall. As Hester crossed the room towards the chiffonier, Kelsey said: 'I'd rather you didn't touch it.' He took from his pocket a clean, folded handkerchief and opened it out. Wrapping it round his fingers, he opened the cupboard of the chiffonier. On the shelf inside was a fancy confectionery box. 'That's it!' Lilian exclaimed. Again with the aid of the handkerchief, Kelsey removed the box, set it down on the table and raised the lid.

Three marrons were missing from one row. The gold-foil wrapping was identical with the square found in Billy's pocket. Kelsey asked who had eaten the three marrons.

'Bridget took one and I gave one to Hester,' Lilian recalled. 'I didn't take one as I was going out to dinner and Robert certainly didn't take one.' She frowned. 'That still leaves one unaccounted for.'

'Did either of you eat one later?' Kelsey asked. 'A day or two later, maybe?'

Lilian shook her head at once. 'I certainly didn't. I'm no great eater of any sort of confectionery.'

'And I didn't take another,' Hester declared. 'I didn't much care for the one I did eat.'

'I suppose Bridget could have taken another after I left,' Lilian conjectured.

Kelsey switched tack. Had either of them recently noticed if any small ornament was missing from the house?

No, neither could recall noticing anything of the sort.

Kelsey offered no explanation for any of these questions but went on to tell Lilian the resumed inquest would not now be concluded on Friday; they would merely apply for a further adjournment. 'There's no reason now for you to attend tomorrow,' he added. In his opinion the body would be released for burial if an application was made.

Lilian drew a long, shuddering breath. 'I thought tomorrow would be the end of it,' she said with a break in her voice. 'I'll have to tell Bridget. She was coming over tomorrow, to go with me. She'll want to know why it's being adjourned again.' Her look of distress deepened.

'We can let Mrs Farrell know, if you'd prefer,' Kelsey offered. 'We'll be having another word with her anyway.'

She looked relieved. 'Yes, please, if you would.' She fell silent for a moment and then asked with some urgency: 'Why is the inquest being adjourned again? You told me it was all straightforward. Has something come up?'

'We feel now,' Kelsey answered flatly, 'that it may not be quite

118

as straightforward as we believed. We feel it needs further investigation.'

She pressed her hands together. 'Why do you think that?' She frowned. 'Why did you ask about the foil? And about the marrons?'

There was a brief silence before Kelsey replied without any expression in his voice: 'The piece of foil I showed you was found in the pocket of the jacket Billy Coleman was wearing when his body was discovered.'

Hester gave a loud gasp. A moment later her expression changed abruptly to one of sudden illumination.

'Billy Coleman?' Lilian echoed. 'What has that got to do with Robert? The boy could have got a marron from anywhere. Just because there's a box in this house it doesn't mean he must have got a marron here.' When Kelsey said nothing she went on: 'Is there any reason – apart from the marron – to suppose the boy was here that evening?' A fresh thought struck her. 'Why did you ask if we'd missed an ornament?'

Kelsey didn't answer any of her questions but asked one of his own: 'Are you aware of any connection, any connection at all, between your husband and Billy Coleman?'

That struck her with the force of a blow. She shook her head without speaking. She looked pale and shocked.

Kelsey turned to Hester, asked if she knew of any connection. She shook her head vigorously.

Lilian suddenly uttered an appalled sound as if some shattering thought had all at once risen up in her brain. But she didn't voice the thought, whatever it might have been. She dropped into a chair and sat with her head in her hands.

'I'd like your permission to have the house dusted for fingerprints,' Kelsey said gently.

She didn't look up, she merely nodded.

'I can get officers round right away,' he added.

Again she nodded.

When Kelsey and Lambert left some time later, Hester walked with them to the front door. She kept her voice down as she said: 'I could see what Mrs Anstey must have been thinking. I wondered the same thing myself. Do you think Mr Anstey might somehow have killed that boy in some kind of dreadful accident, without meaning to? And then when he realized what he'd done he went and killed himself?' She stared up into his face. 'Is that what you think? Can it possibly be true?'

Kelsey made no reply.

'Poor Mrs Anstey!' She wrung her hands, her face creased in anguish.

In the car on the way back to the station Lambert said: 'It's not impossible. Billy gets into the house, Anstey comes across him, grabs hold of him, kills him by accident. Anstey's already in a low state, he's been having thoughts of suicide. Coming on top of his illness, the accident is the last straw, it pushes him over the edge.'

Kelsey offered no response and Lambert said nothing more.

DC Slade was sent straight over to Wychford to let Bridget Farrell know about the further adjournment of the inquest and to ask if she had eaten a second marron that Friday evening.

She appeared greatly surprised at the news of the inquest and much puzzled by the question about the marrons. No, she definitely had not eaten a second marron nor had she seen Uncle Robert take one. She appeared equally surprised and baffled by the constable's next questions: Did she have any knowledge of Billy Coleman's presence in Kincraig that Friday evening? Did she know of any connection between Billy and Robert Anstey?

Her answer to both questions was an emphatic no. She pressed Slade for some explanation of all this but he made no attempt to satisfy her curiosity. Her bafflement was further increased when Slade informed her he was under instruction to take her fingerprints and those of her husband. He did offer an explanation for this when she insisted on knowing the reason. 'For purposes of elimination,' he told her. She then submitted with a bad grace.

Keith Farrell had sat by all this time, listening intently but making no comment, asking no questions; he made no protest now at having his prints taken.

Later, alone in his office, Kelsey sat down to consider with the full beam of concentration the question that had earlier crossed his own mind, had been voiced by Hester Whiting and echoed by Sergeant Lambert: Could Robert Anstey have accidentally killed Billy Coleman before taking his own life?

Some time later still he answered the question to his own satisfaction: the answer was a categoric no. Nothing in what he knew of Anstey's nature even remotely suggested that he was a man capable of a violent outburst of temper, let alone capable of killing, even by accident, a child he came across in his house. Whoever killed Billy had been very determined to put an end to the boy's life.

The phone call to Hibberd and the arrangement about the contract that Anstey had made with Lilian that Friday morning, these two facts, plus the other attendant details of Anstey's death, all went to confirm the theory of a carefully thought out suicide, planned well in advance. Nothing about Anstey's death suggested some last-minute, panic-stricken impulse, some hastily improvised self-killing.

Lastly, and most convincing of all, to his mind, the post-mortem staining of Billy's body showed beyond a shadow of doubt that the body had lain on its back for some hours before being dumped in Crowswood. The timings simply couldn't be made to square with the notion of Anstey as Billy's killer.

20

Inquiries of both Glenna Coleman and Billy's friend, David Willcox – still convalescing at home – failed to reveal any connection between Billy and Robert Anstey. Glenna appeared deeply puzzled by the question but was given no explanation.

After the conference and briefing on Friday morning Kelsey spent some time studying the results of the Kincraig fingerprint dusting. Billy's prints had been found on the box of marrons, on one side of a window-frame in Anstey's study and on a back-door jamb, this last suggesting one hand being placed on the door-frame while silently easing the door shut with the other hand, after stepping inside the house.

Kelsey dispatched DC Slade to Kincraig to have a word with the gardener, Liggitt. Slade didn't go up to the house but followed the sound of activity to where Liggitt was at work among the rose beds. He asked the gardener if he had ever seen Billy Coleman at Kincraig, if he knew of any connection, however slight, between Billy and Robert Anstey. He didn't need to produce a photograph; in common with the majority of Cannonbridge citizens Liggitt was familiar with Billy's face from newspapers and TV.

The questions, with all their implications, astonished and horrified Liggitt. No, he replied at once, he had never seen Billy in or about Kincraig, nor did he know of any connection between Billy and Mr Anstey. He looked as if he would dearly like to know the reason for these questions but he managed to restrain the impulse to inquire.

As Slade turned to go, Liggitt suddenly asked: 'That business at Paragon, calling in the auditors to go through the accounts, do you happen to know if they're going to prosecute Matt Shardlow?'

'I couldn't tell you,' Slade replied. 'My guess, for what it's worth, is that it's up to Mrs Anstey now. Do you know Shardlow?'

Liggitt moved his shoulders. 'I don't know him personally but I've known him by sight for years. My wife has a nephew working at Paragon, he told us about the investigation, about Shardlow being suspended.' He hesitated and then continued in a rush: 'A few weeks back I saw Shardlow calling in here, at the house. I spoke to Mrs Whiting about it and she more or less shut me up. She got on her high horse, she said he'd only called the once and that was on Paragon business. But I noticed she coloured up. And I'd definitely seen him here three times with my own eyes. It didn't seem very likely to me he'd be calling on Paragon business after he'd been suspended. And why would he call at a time when he'd know full well Mr Anstey wasn't likely to be here?'

He gave a meaningful jerk of his head. 'Something else I'd noticed: she'd started smartening herself up, she'd had her hair done, had it tinted. I'd no wish to go interfering in her private life, and if she'd got herself a boyfriend, well, she's a widow, so why not? Good luck to her is what I'd say in the ordinary way, but not if the new boyfriend was Matt Shardlow and he'd taken to dropping in at Kincraig. I was pretty certain Mr and Mrs

Anstey wouldn't be best pleased if they knew he was in and out of the house when their backs were turned. So I said to her straight out that I didn't think it was right for her to have him in the place when the Ansteys weren't here.' He made a face. 'She didn't like that at all. She wanted to know what I was implying. I just said I'd no wish to be offensive. I didn't intend to go on about it, I'd leave it to her own good sense. And she said: "Yes, you do that." Give her her due, I've never seen Shardlow here again after I spoke to her.'

'When would that be, that you spoke to her?' Slade inquired.

Liggitt thought back. 'I suppose it would be about three weeks ago. I don't know Mrs Whiting very well, she hasn't been here all that long and she isn't one to say a lot about herself. But from what I do know of her, my guess is Matt Shardlow could run rings round her.'

When Slade got back to the station the Chief was about to leave for the courthouse but he took a few minutes to hear what Slade had to tell him, showing particular interest in what Liggitt had said about Matt Shardlow's calls at Kincraig. The Chief then sent Slade straight out again, this time to call on Shardlow, take his fingerprints.

The inquest proceedings were soon over. A further adjournment was granted, Anstey's body was released for burial.

A little after midday Lambert drove the Chief round to Kincraig. They didn't go near Liggitt but pressed the front doorbell to summon Mrs Whiting.

'Mrs Anstey isn't here,' she told the Chief as soon as she opened the door. 'She's at the works, she won't be home till five thirty.'

'It isn't Mrs Anstey we've come to see,' Kelsey responded. 'It's you we'd like a word with.'

She looked surprised but said nothing; she took them along to the sitting-room. When Kelsey invited her to sit down she perched herself stiffly on an upright chair. He wasted no time but asked if she was acquainted with Matthew Shardlow.

She held herself even more tensely; the colour began a slow rise in her cheeks. By way of reply she gave a little nod.

How long had she known him? How had the acquaintance come about?

She shifted slightly. She didn't look at Kelsey but stared down

123

at the carpet. She told him she had known Shardlow a few weeks. He had called at the house asking to speak to Mr Anstey who was not in at the time. It was a cold day. She had been about to have coffee and she had offered Shardlow a cup. They had got chatting.

And after that?

He had called at Kincraig in passing, once or twice, just for a chat and a cup of coffee. Later he had asked her out.

'Did he tell you he'd been suspended from Paragon? That a fraud inquiry was going forward?'

'Yes, he did,' she replied at once. 'He was very straight, very open, right from the first.'

'Did he ask if you knew what Mr Anstey intended doing? If he intended prosecuting?'

She frowned. 'What if he did? There was no harm in that. I couldn't help hearing what was said when I was serving supper or clearing the table. Mr and Mrs Anstey often talked about business at the table.'

'And you told Shardlow what you knew?'

She bit her lip. 'I just passed on a few bits of information. I couldn't see any harm in that, he'd be bound to know sooner or later.' A note of defiance sounded in her voice. 'I thought he had a right to know if he was going to be accused of something he hadn't done.'

'You were sure he'd done nothing wrong?'

'Yes, of course. When he explained it all to me I was quite certain Mr Anstey had misjudged him. Matthew told me he'd had nothing to do with any muddle in the books. And it wasn't fraud on Ted Gilchrist's part. Ted would never have got up to anything dishonest, he was just getting past it and he sometimes made mistakes. Matthew had had to rescue him before but he just happened to be away on holiday when Ted died. He was knocked sideways when he got back and discovered Ted was dead and they'd got a fraud inquiry going. Mr Anstey never gave him a chance to say one word, he just threw him out. Matt was sure – and so was I, when he explained everything – it would all soon be cleared up and he'd be back at work again.'

'How often did Shardlow call here to see you?'

She didn't have to think back. 'Three times,' she replied promptly. 'After that he called at my house.'

'When he called here, which part of the house did he go into?'

'Only the kitchen – and once, the bathroom.'

'Nowhere else? You're sure?'

'Quite sure. He had no reason to go anywhere else.'

'Are you still seeing him?'

'Yes, I am.'

'When was the last time you went out with him?'

She hesitated. 'We haven't actually been out together since Mr Anstey died. It was a terrible shock for both of us. We haven't either of us felt much like going out since it happened.'

'But he's in touch with you?'

Again she hesitated. She opened her mouth and then closed it again.

'Does he phone you?' Kelsey pressed her.

She shook her head.

'When did you last lay eyes on him?'

Again, she didn't have to think back, she was able to supply the answer instantly: 'He called round to my house to say how upset he was at Mr Anstey's death and what a shock it must have been for me. He said he'd be in touch when we both felt steadier.'

'When was this?'

'On the Monday evening after Mr Anstey died. He said he'd called earlier, on the Sunday morning, and got no reply – I was round here, of course, giving Mrs Anstey a hand.' She fell silent for a moment and then burst out in tones of quiet intensity: 'He's made a wonderful difference to my life.' She fell silent again, looking across at Kelsey with earnest appeal, her face working. 'You won't tell Mrs Anstey about Matt and me, will you? *Please!* She doesn't know anything about it, she has no idea he was ever inside the house. If you tell her she'll be upset, I know she will. I'll lose my job. And she needs me, you know she does.'

He regarded her for a long moment before giving, by way of reply, a non-committal grunt. But her expression relaxed marginally, as if she could read into that something not totally devoid of hope.

Later in the day, on no fewer than three separate occasions, Kelsey gave orders to have Shardlow brought into the station but on none of the three occasions did the officers find Shardlow at home.

In the evening DC Slade went round to old Mrs Shardlow's cottage, expecting, the day being Friday, to find him there.

But he wasn't there. His mother made her way slowly along to the door to answer Slade's ring. She cupped her hand behind her ear, leaning forward. 'I'll have to ask you to speak up,' she said with an apologetic smile. 'My hearing isn't too good these days.'

She told him Matt had rung her around teatime to say he wouldn't be calling in this evening, he had a bit of business to attend to. He'd be around to see her sometime tomorrow.

Slade asked if he might take a look at the workshop and she made no objection. She took him along a passage, opened a door and switched on a light, illuminating a flight of steps.

'I won't come down with you,' she told him, apologetic again. 'I haven't been down there in a long while. My knees aren't what they used to be.' She went slowly back to the living-room and Slade descended the steps.

The workshop looked efficient and well set up. There were items of old furniture in various stages of repair. A door led out into the garden. He opened it and stepped outside.

Nearby was an area of hard-standing. If Shardlow had parked his car there that Friday evening, he could have left the basement, got into his car, slid it quietly out and away, returning later to restore the car to its position before stepping back into the workshop, occupying himself there for an interval, short or long as suited him, and then mounting the stairs back into the house, to sit chatting to his mother, make her a bedtime drink; all this without his mother being in any way aware of his temporary absence. And there would have been nothing to stop him, after he said good-night and left the cottage, making a detour before driving back to his house, a detour that could have taken him out to Crowswood, to rid himself there of some burden that might have been lying for the past few hours in his vehicle.

Matt Shardlow was at home at breakfast time next morning when the police called yet again. He made no demur about accompanying them to the station.

The Chief began the interview briskly. 'I understand you have formed an association with Mrs Hester Whiting, the housekeeper at Kincraig.'

Shardlow smiled. 'Formed an association isn't exactly the way I'd put it. I've become friendly with her, if that's what you mean.'

'On the occasions when you called at Kincraig, which rooms in the house did you enter?'

Shardlow sat back in his chair, he appeared completely at ease. 'Let me see now. I went into the kitchen. And once I went upstairs into the bathroom.'

'No other room?'

He shook his head.

'Then how come,' Kelsey asked, 'we've found two good clear prints of yours in Mr Anstey's study?'

Shardlow raised a hand. 'You're right, I'd forgotten that. I did go into the study. It was on my way back from the bathroom. When I got downstairs again, I couldn't resist nipping into the study for a moment.'

'What was your object in going in?'

He moved his shoulders. 'I suppose I had some sort of half-baked notion I might see some papers lying on the desk, papers about the fraud inquiry at Paragon, I might get some clue about what Mr Anstey intended doing about it.' He smiled again. 'Of course there were no papers lying about.'

'Now that Mr Anstey's dead,' Kelsey said, 'do you expect a case to be brought against you?'

Shardlow pursed his lips. 'I rather think not,' he replied with a judicial air. 'I believe Mrs Anstey is against it.'

'So as far as you're concerned, Mr Anstey's death has been a stroke of good luck.'

He inclined his head. 'It's a pretty drastic way of putting it but I suppose you could say that.'

'Did you set foot inside Kincraig on the evening of Friday, 25th October?'

Shardlow gave a vigorous headshake. 'I most certainly did not.'

'Did you at any place, at any time on the evening of Friday, 25th October, come across Billy Coleman?'

Another vigorous headshake. 'No, I did not.'

Kelsey switched tack abruptly. 'Do you intend to go on seeing Mrs Whiting?'

127

Shardlow pulled down the corners of his mouth. 'I really couldn't say. Mr Anstey's death has put a damper on things. We'll have to see how it goes.'

Another swift change of tack. 'Could we have the address of your ex-wife?'

That brought him up sharp. For the first time he looked rattled. There was a brief silence before he replied in a truculent tone: 'What do you want to talk to her for? I haven't seen her in a long while. She knows nothing about what I'm doing these days. She's got a life of her own now, she won't thank you for trying to bring her into this.'

'If we could just have the address,' Kelsey persisted. 'Then you're free to leave.'

There was a further brief silence, then Shardlow drew a long, irritated breath and supplied the address.

After the door had closed behind him Kelsey sat for some time with his chin propped on his hand. Something that had been niggling away in the depths of his mind was now pushing its way stubbornly, inexorably upwards. Something in the toxicology report on Anstey: the undissolved capsule swallowed by Anstey along with the sleeping-pills and the hot milky drink. The prescribed dosage was one capsule three times daily. The capsules contained medication intended to alleviate the symptoms of Anstey's illness over the long term; they produced no immediate or short-term effect; they could contribute nothing to drowsiness or to the tranquillity of final moments.

Kelsey had never been entirely happy about that capsule but with everything pointing so conclusively to suicide he had persuaded himself that Anstey had reached for the bottle as he reached for it every night, he had automatically tipped out one capsule and swallowed it.

Now he was not so sure. A highly intelligent, highly organized man like Anstey, every other detail of the suicide clearly thought out, why that one little touch of inadvertence?

He found it possible now to see it in quite another light: Anstey had simply swallowed the capsule in the course of his ordinary routine of scrupulously following doctor's orders, in his faith in the efficacy of such long-term palliative medication, in his belief that he would live long enough to benefit from it –

128

nothing further from his mind at that moment than any thought of doing away with himself.

In which case it must have been some other person who tampered with the contents of the beverage jar or the sugar bowl or both, lacing the top layer of one or both with powdered sleeping-pills. It must have been some other person who placed the plastic bag over Anstey's head, after he had fallen into a sedated slumber, some other person who slipped the magazine cutting under the radio, attended to what had to be done in bedroom and kitchen to make sure nothing quarrelled with the concept of suicide.

He got to his feet and crossed to the window, he stood staring out. Was it conceivable that Anstey's death might not after all have been suicide but murder dressed up to look like suicide?

21

Monday morning was crisp and bright. Billy Coleman's funeral was set down for eleven thirty at the small church near the Westway estate, the church where his parents had been married, where Billy had been christened, where he had attended Sunday school in earlier years, the church where his mother was buried. There was room in her grave for the small white coffin holding the remains of the son who had loved her so dearly.

The funeral was, as expected, a high-profile media event, with large crowds lining the route. The little church was filled to overflowing with wreaths and flowers. The head teacher and class teacher brought with them the children from Billy's class; the only member of the class not present was David Willcox, still said to be convalescing at home. In the absence of any relatives the coffin was borne by the fathers of two of Billy's classmates. There was no sign of Lew Dutton or Tom Palmer, no sign of Matthew Shardlow.

Residents from the Westway estate came in force; neither of the Willcox parents figured among them. Kelsey had detailed DC Slade to drive Glenna Coleman and Edna Quirke to the church, remain with them throughout the service, drive them back to Edna's cottage when it was all over. The three of them sat together in a pew right at the back.

Kelsey managed a word with Glenna at the end, as the three were about to leave for the cottage. Glenna appeared restless and despondent. She told him she was finding it increasingly difficult to occupy herself. 'I know I can't leave this area for the present,' she acknowledged, 'but the moment I'm free to go I'll be off like a shot, somewhere where no one knows me. Some big city where I'll be swallowed up in the crowds.' She would be beginning again from scratch, as she had done more than once before in her life. She had run away from home at fifteen, she had no family worth speaking of.

Matthew Shardlow's ex-wife was now the manageress of a dry-cleaning shop in a town some twenty-five miles from Cannon-bridge; she occupied the flat above the shop. Kelsey arranged to see her before the start of business on Tuesday morning and promptly at five minutes to eight Sergeant Lambert drew up nearby.

Matthew's ex-wife was a smartly dressed, good-looking woman in her mid-thirties with an easy manner, an air of energy and competence. Kelsey had given her over the phone an indication of why he wished to talk to her and she held herself ready to answer his questions without loss of time.

He plunged straight in. Had she found Matthew Shardlow to be a man of violent temper?

Yes, she could say that. Not habitually violent but given to occasional outbursts when he was liable to strike out, sometimes on slight provocation. Chiefly on this account the marriage had teetered on the brink for some time before the break-up; it had finally ended when Shardlow had lashed out once too often.

She hadn't made his treatment of her the grounds for divorce. She had loved him once; she had liked and respected his mother; she had her pride. For all these reasons she preferred to wait and approach Shardlow in due course for a divorce by consent. When the time arrived he raised no objection. She had asked for only nominal alimony but had insisted on a half-share of the value of the house; Shardlow had agreed to this only after strenuous resistance.

Although she no longer had any contact with her ex-husband she still kept in touch with friends from her time in Cannonbridge and was aware of Shardlow's suspension from Paragon and the rumours arising from it. No, she couldn't say she had been surprised to learn he was suspected of fraud, nor would she be surprised to learn at some future date that he had somehow contrived to wriggle free of any charge.

As they got back into the car Sergeant Lambert observed: 'It's hard to believe Shardlow could have been genuinely attracted to Hester Whiting. She's not in the same league as his ex-wife.'

Shortly after lunch Lambert drove the Chief to the offices of the auditors carrying out the fraud investigation. Kelsey questioned them closely about what they believed to be the specific part played in the fraud by each of the two men, Gilchrist and Shardlow, and what they had learned of each man's background and motivation.

On leaving the auditors they drove to Hester Whiting's house, finding her at home, taking her afternoon break from her duties at Kincraig.

Without any preamble Kelsey addressed the matter of her relationship with Shardlow. She held herself tensely throughout, her forehead all the while creased in a frown.

Had Shardlow ever asked her about the household routine at Kincraig? Did he want to know if Mrs Anstey went out on her own in the evenings, what time Mr Anstey went to bed, if Mr Anstey was in the habit of taking a drink of any kind before bed? Did he inquire about her own routine in setting out the bedtime tray for Mr Anstey?

She twisted her hands as she replied. She and Matthew had certainly chatted about things in a casual fashion. In the course of ordinary conversation she may have spoken of such matters but there had never been any detailed questioning of the kind the Chief was suggesting. It was no more than friendly interest on Matthew's part.

Kelsey switched tack. Had she left the back door at Kincraig unsecured that Friday evening, or any other evening?

'No, of course not!' she exclaimed in sharp indignation. 'I'd never do such a thing! Why on earth would I?'

131

'Maybe Shardlow suggested he might slip in to talk to Mr Anstey while Mrs Anstey was out at the dinner. Or he might get a chance to take a good look round the study after Mr Anstey was in bed, see if he could find any papers about the fraud inquiry.'

'Matthew never suggested any such thing!' she retorted with heat. 'It would have been a mad idea to try to talk to Mr Anstey by sneaking into the house that way. Mr Anstey would immediately have thrown him out – or sent for the police to charge him. Matthew would know that, he's not a fool.' She leaned forward, fixing the Chief with her gaze. 'The back door must have been properly locked and bolted when I got to Kincraig that Saturday morning after Mr Anstey died. I'd certainly have noticed if I'd found it any different from usual.'

'You're telling me,' Kelsey said, 'that with all the upset of that morning, the early phone call from Mrs Anstey, the dreadful news of Mr Anstey's death, the fact that you had to change your plans for the day at a moment's notice, with all that going on, you can be absolutely certain you would have noticed, when you got to Kincraig, if the back door was not as you left it the previous evening?'

Her manner deflated suddenly and she made no reply. When Kelsey asked if they might look through her things she sat in silence for some moments, she looked stunned at the notion. At last she gave a single nod. She didn't go with them from room to room but stayed where she was until the search was finished. It yielded nothing.

She didn't go with them to the door when they left but remained in the same position, wearing the same stunned air.

The two policemen went down the path to the car. As Kelsey reached for the door handle a sudden thought halted him: what of the phone call made by Anstey to Stephen Hibberd that Friday evening? How did that fit in with the conjectures concerning Shardlow and Hester Whiting currently flitting about in his brain?

He got into the car, leaned back and closed his eyes. By the time the car drew up on the station forecourt he had answered himself: there was no conceivable way in which that phone call could be made to square with any theory of Shardlow, with or without the aid – intentional or unintentional – of Hester Whiting, being active in what had happened – whatever that might be – at Kincraig that Friday evening.

22

The funeral of Robert James Anstey was arranged for three o'clock on Wednesday afternoon. The works shut down at lunch-time and at two thirty the workforce assembled, entirely by agreement among themselves, before the main building and set off in orderly procession for the church – the largest and oldest church in Cannonbridge. Robert would be buried beside his first wife, next to the graves of her parents.

As was to be expected, reporters were present from local and county newspapers but there were also two or three from national dailies. During the morning's news conference on the Billy Coleman case, it was plain that the national media had got wind of a possible connection between Billy's death and that of Robert Anstey. Some very pointed questions were asked but Kelsey had managed to field them all.

Representatives of many organizations and clubs attended the funeral. There was a considerable turnout of local dignitaries, professional and business friends and colleagues, an impressive array of wreaths and flowers.

Lilian Anstey bore up well. She was accompanied by the Joslins, with the Farrells close by and solicitous throughout. Mrs Whiting came with Liggitt and his wife, together with an older woman whom Liggitt introduced to the Chief: Miss Newsome, who had been housekeeper to Mr Anstey until the summer. She had come up from the Devon seaside resort to which she had retired, especially to attend the funeral; she appeared deeply saddened at the passing of her old employer. Kelsey was surprised to see how fit and vigorous she looked, scarcely ready for retirement.

In the throng he caught a glimpse of Stephen Hibberd and his wife. Nowhere was there any sign of Matthew Shardlow.

When it was all over and Kelsey went back to his office, one image persisted in his brain: Bridget Farrell, so solicitous, dancing unflagging attendance on Lilian Anstey. A false note there, he couldn't help feeling.

He sat drumming his fingers on his desk. Bridget had visited Kincraig that Friday evening; she had also called in there two days earlier, on the Wednesday. She had remained in the house, alone with Robert, on the Friday evening, for an undetermined length of time. She had come into a substantial legacy on Robert's death, a legacy she was free to use entirely as she pleased, a legacy Robert might, had he lived only a little longer, have cancelled or hedged about with restrictions.

Could Bridget possibly have known he was contemplating altering his will? She worked in a solicitor's office, had worked there for years. Was it conceivable she could have learned through some kind of grapevine of Anstey's phone call to his solicitor's office the morning after that Sunday tea party when Robert had turned down the Farrells' request for money?

Another image flashed into his brain: Sylvie Murchison, secretary to Cartwright, Anstey's solicitor, nervously plucking at the sleeve of her jacket as she sat facing him, answering his questions, in Cartwright's office. Could she be a friend of Bridget's? Could Sylvie, intentionally or unwittingly, have alerted Bridget to Anstey's phone call and its possible implications?

The more he thought about it the more he saw that a word with Miss Sylvie Murchison might not come amiss.

A constable's endeavours via the phone book and the electoral register revealed that a Mrs Emily Murchison and a Miss Sylvie Murchison lived at Maitland Villa, in a residential suburb of Cannonbridge.

Lambert drove the Chief over to the villa at five forty-five. Sylvie Murchison opened the door to them, still in her outdoor clothes; she had just got in from work. At the sight of the two men a look of alarm flashed across her face. She at once came out on to the step, almost closing the door behind her.

The Chief indicated that he would be glad of a few minutes of her time, he had some questions to put to her. She didn't ask the nature of the questions but responded with an urgent: 'Yes, very well, but not here, please. My mother's here. She's old, she's easily upset. I'd far rather speak to you at the police station. I'll just pop back in and tell her I have to go out.'

She joined them in their car a few minutes later. She remained in uneasy silence until they were all seated in an interview room at the police station.

Kelsey began by asking if she was acquainted with Mrs Bridget Farrell.

'Yes, I am,' she replied dully, with the air of one who knows with certainty that something unpleasant is coming.

Had she ever discussed with Bridget any details of any will of Robert Anstey's?

She said nothing. She looked on the verge of tears.

'I could ask you these questions in the presence of your employer, Mr Cartwright,' Kelsey pointed out. She sprang up in the chair in shock, subsiding after a moment.

'If I tell you what I know,' she said tremulously, 'do you intend to tell Mr Cartwright about it?'

'I can't give any cast-iron guarantees,' Kelsey told her. 'Circumstances might force me to tell him, though I don't think that's very likely. All I can say is that it's not my intention to tell him.'

She drew a long breath and gave a couple of slow nods. 'Very well, then. I accept that in good faith.' She hesitated. 'I'm not proud of any of this.' She went on in a stumbling fashion to explain how she had got herself into a situation some time back whereby Bridget Farrell had been able to do her a favour, helped her cover up an error of some importance. Bridget hadn't hesitated thereafter to ask for favours in return, chiefly concerned with the passing on of full details of Robert Anstey's will, together with any changes or proposed changes in the will.

'So Bridget knew the full contents of both the wills Anstey made?' Kelsey said.

She nodded. 'She rang me early in October to ask if Mr Anstey had made an appointment to see Mr Cartwright.' She had told Bridget Mr Anstey had indeed rung the office a few days earlier. When he was informed that Cartwright was away on holiday he said he'd ring again after Cartwright got back. Bridget had asked if Mr Anstey had indicated why he wanted to see Cartwright and Sylvie told her it was to seek advice about possible changes to his will.

When Sergeant Lambert drove the Chief over to Wychford, they took with them an extra driver, to allow them to take in both the Farrells' cars for scrutiny.

The Farrells had finished their evening meal, had cleared up and were about to sit down when the doorbell rang. It was Keith who answered the door. He showed no surprise at the sight of the two policemen, no reluctance to admit them. He assured them their visit wasn't in the least inconvenient; neither he nor his wife had any engagement for the evening.

By this time Bridget had come out into the hallway. Her manner was composed and affable. She offered refreshment, which the Chief declined.

When they were all settled in the living-room the Chief began by asking at what time Bridget had returned home that Friday evening, after visiting Kincraig.

At around eight fifteen, eight twenty, he was told; both husband and wife were agreed on that.

How had they spent the remainder of that evening?

Again, no difficulty in recall by either of them. They had both spent the evening at home, neither had at any time left the house. They had gone to bed around eleven.

The Chief's next questions were directed at Bridget. Had she gone along to the Kincraig kitchen at any time during her visit that Friday evening or during her Wednesday visit, two days earlier?

Her answer for both evenings was a decisive no.

Why had she decided to visit Kincraig twice in that one week?

A swift, easy reply: a woman friend living in Wychford had had to go into the Cannonbridge hospital. Bridget had visited her straight from work on both days and had taken the opportunity afterwards to look in on Uncle Robert, see how he was. She supplied unasked the name and address of her friend, now out of hospital and back home.

Kelsey switched tack. Had she been aware before Robert Anstey's death of the contents of either of his wills?

She shook her head at once. Uncle Robert had told her he was leaving her a substantial legacy but apart from that she had known nothing and would in fact have considered it none of her business. If she had given the matter any thought she would have imagined that the bulk of the estate would go to Lilian, as indeed it did.

Had she been aware of a phone call made by Anstey to his solicitor's office at the end of September, in which he had indicated that he wanted to discuss possible changes to his will?

Again she shook her head. She had known nothing of any such phone call.

Kelsey studied her in silence. 'My belief is,' he said at last, 'that you knew in exact detail the contents of both Anstey's wills and that you also knew what was said during that phone call to Cartwright's office.'

'Then your belief is mistaken,' she retorted.

Kelsey asked if either she or her husband had been in any kind of money difficulty in recent months.

Once more she shook her head. 'No difficulties at all,' she assured him. He was welcome to scrutinize their bank accounts. She glanced at her husband who spoke up at once in agreement. They supplied details of their accounts.

Kelsey then asked if they might look through the Farrells' things. There were some moments of tense silence before they gave their permission. A quick inspection revealed nothing of interest.

Kelsey went on to inform them that he would be taking both their cars in for examination, the cars would be returned as soon as possible.

This news also was received in tense silence. At last Keith gave a nod, still without speaking.

'I don't know what all this is in aid of,' Bridget suddenly burst out. 'Any more than I know why the inquest on Uncle Robert was adjourned again.' She paused and then added with a needling air: 'You seem mighty interested in picking up all kinds of information, you might be interested in one or two facts we've picked up ourselves, facts about dear Madame Lilian.' Her tone was shot through with spiteful pleasure. She leaned forward, a little smile played about her lips. 'We were rather curious about our dear Lilian. Keith asked me about her and I realized I knew almost nothing about her background, her previous marriage. We decided it might be an idea to find out a little more about her. So we went to a private inquiry agent a few months ago and got him to make some inquiries.'

Kelsey asked if the agent was a local man.

'No, he wasn't.' She mentioned the name of an agent in a

neighbouring town. 'He did a good job, gave us a very full report.' Her eyes glittered with malice. 'It certainly opened our eyes to Madame Lilian. She didn't get what she wanted from her first marriage so she set off to try her luck again. This time she was looking for a man with more money than her first husband and no children to put a spoke in the wheel. She had better luck the second time around, this time she's got what she wanted.'

'Bridget's certainly no friend of Lilian's,' Sergeant Lambert observed to Kelsey on the way back to Cannonbridge. 'I don't know that I'd care to have her for an enemy.'

When the Chief availed himself next morning of the Farrells' permission to scrutinize their bank accounts, he found no indication of any money difficulties on the part of either husband or wife. Later in the morning he sent DC Slade on a double errand: to make inquiries of the woman friend Bridget claimed to have visited in hospital and to try, if he could, to shake the Farrells' statement of how they had spent that Friday evening.

It was turned eleven when Slade located the house belonging to Bridget's friend. A pleasant-looking woman in early middle age came to the door in answer to his ring. Yes, she had recently been in the Cannonbridge hospital; she was there from 21st October to the 28th; she was still convalescing. And yes, Bridget had called to see her there on both the Wednesday and Friday evenings. She looked as if she would dearly like to inquire about the reason for these questions. But she didn't ask and Slade didn't enlighten her.

He went next to the estate where the Farrells lived. The road where their house stood was not very long. He called at every dwelling on both sides to put the question: had anyone seen either of the Farrells or either of their cars returning to or leaving their house that Friday evening? At several of the dwellings he found no one at home. When he did find someone the answer was in every case the same: the best part of three weeks had gone by since that evening and no one could now recall with any certainty such a trivial happening so far back.

It was twelve thirty as he got back into his car, far from pleased with his efforts. He was about to switch on the ignition when he saw a cyclist, a girl of fifteen or sixteen in school uniform, turn into the driveway of a house where he had called a few minutes earlier; he had spoken to a woman there who had been unable to help him.

In a spirit of dogged determination he got out of his car and went back to the house. When the same woman answered his ring he apologized for troubling her again; he mentioned the girl he had just seen. 'That's my daughter,' the woman told him. 'She's come home for her lunch.' Yes, he was welcome to speak to her.

She took him along to the kitchen where the girl was just about to sit down at the table. He put his question to her and she thought back.

She had no difficulty in recalling that particular Friday. She had made a tour of the estate that evening, with a boy from the same form at school, attempting to drum up support for a sponsored swim in which they would both be taking part, the proceeds to go to the local hospital scanner appeal.

She well remembered their call at the Farrells' house. Mr Farrell had answered the door. He had agreed to sponsor them both, putting his name down for a generous amount. Mrs Farrell had come to the door as they were ready to leave. She had added her name to the list, matching the sum promised by her husband. Both the Farrells had stood chatting to them about the event for some minutes. The girl was pretty certain of the time: it would be around nine o'clock.

In the early evening Kelsey went along to Kincraig to ask Lilian Anstey if he might address the Paragon workforce during the lunch hour next day; he wouldn't take long. He didn't indicate the nature of what he intended saying and Lilian didn't ask, though she appeared surprised at the request. 'Yes, of course,' she responded. 'Anything at all you need to do, that you feel might be helpful.'

The scrutiny of the Farrells' cars proved negative and towards the end of Friday morning the Chief gave instructions for both cars to be returned.

Lilian Anstey had arranged for him to address the Paragon

workforce in the canteen immediately before lunch; the break would be extended by twenty minutes, to allow those who normally ate elsewhere to be present.

Lilian introduced him in a manner suggestive of iron self-control and then took her place beside him. All the time he spoke she looked straight ahead at the opposite wall, with an expressionless face.

He came straight to the point. The death of Billy Coleman had taken place on the same evening as the death of Robert Anstey and it was now thought possible that there might have been some connection between the two deaths. A sharp stir of interest, a low ripple of sound, ran through the audience. If anyone present knew of any link, however slight, between Billy and Robert Anstey, the Chief was most anxious to hear of it.

He made a renewed appeal for any other information, however insignificant-seeming, about either of the two deaths, the events of that Friday evening, or any happening around that time that might conceivably have some bearing on what had taken place.

He said not a word to give the least hint that he was now turning over in his mind the possibility that Anstey's death had not been suicide but murder.

There was no immediate response and the Chief had expected none. But he had hopes that something might result before the end of the day; someone might call into the station or make a phone call on the way home from work.

But that time came and passed. No one called in, no one rang.

Shortly after seven thirty, as he was about to knock off for the night, someone entered the building and approached the front desk, asking to speak to him. A young woman, giving her name as Delphine Tate, an office worker at Paragon.

She had, it seemed, struggled with herself all afternoon as to whether or not she should come forward. By the time she put on her coat at the end of the day she had made up her mind to say nothing. If it came out that she had spoken, she might lose her job. And what she had to say would in all probability be written off as valueless by the police. She had gone back to her flat, eaten her supper, washed up, tidied up, switched on the TV, tried to read the evening paper.

It was all no use. At seven fifteen, without conscious volition, she had thrown down the newspaper, got to her feet, switched off the TV, put on her coat and left the flat, heading for the police station.

When it came to the point of what it was she had to tell them, she fell silent. 'It's probably nothing,' she said at last. 'It's all a mistake. I should never have come here.' She half made to rise but Kelsey waved her down again. He encouraged her gently to say whatever it was, let him be the judge of whether or not it had any value.

She took a deep breath and began. 'It's about Ian Bryant.' She saw the name meant nothing to him. 'Ian Bryant,' she said again. 'He worked at Paragon for a few months, a temporary job, a fill-in while he was waiting to go on somewhere else. He worked as a personal assistant, mostly for Mr Anstey but also for Mrs Anstey. Mr Anstey thought a lot of him. He'd have liked him to stay on but he'd got this other job fixed up before he came to Paragon. He left Paragon five weeks ago.' She fell silent again.

'What sort of person is this Ian Bryant?' Kelsey asked. 'What age is he?'

She found her voice again, her words came out in a rush. 'He's single. Twenty-eight. Tall, quite good-looking. I was on holiday when he started working at Paragon. He'd been there a couple of weeks by the time I got back. He was well settled in by then, he'd made himself very useful to Mr and Mrs Anstey.'

She took another deep breath. 'I won't beat about the bush. I really fancied him – to tell the truth, I still do. I was positive he fancied me, and I'm not usually wrong about these things. But I could never get him to ask me out, however much I tried – and I did try, believe you me, I tried everything I knew. He was always very pleasant, friendly enough, but never anything more.' She smiled slightly. 'I don't usually have any trouble, it's usually a case of having to fight them off.' She shook her head slowly. 'There was something about him, I was set on having him.'

'I have a friend in Personnel and she let me see his file so I could check he wasn't married. I knew he wasn't taking out any other girl from Paragon, I made it my business to find out. And for sure he wasn't gay, I couldn't be wrong about that. I thought maybe he already had a girlfriend somewhere else, before he came to Paragon, but when we got chatting I managed to winkle that out of him: he didn't have any steady girlfriend.'

She paused again, she gave the Chief a direct look. 'And then one day I came on him and Mrs Anstey standing together in a corridor and the moment I saw them I knew: he'd got a thing going with Mrs Anstey.' She held up a hand. 'I know. I know exactly what you're going to say: I've no proof, no facts, just the way they were looking at each other, just that one moment. I never saw it again but I was sure all the same. It all made sense.' She gave another faint smile. 'It didn't stop me trying, though, but it was no use. I ran into him in the street a few days after he left Paragon. I couldn't resist trying my luck again. I thought with him leaving, that could be the end of it between him and Lilian. But he still wouldn't play, so I guessed it was still going on.'

She leaned forward, an intense expression on her face. 'Don't you see? Mr Anstey must have found out about them. That's why he killed himself, I'm sure of it. He'd have been pretty depressed anyway, on account of his illness. And then finding out about his wife and Ian Bryant, that must have been the last straw.'

23

Kelsey asked if Delphine knew Ian Bryant's address.

No, she didn't know but she knew where he was now working.

Did she know anything of his background? His home town?

Ian had never been very forthcoming in that regard, she told him. But his file had given her the name of the school he had attended: a state comprehensive in a town forty-five miles away.

Had she by any chance a photograph of Ian?

Yes, she had, a very clear photograph, a very good likeness. The local MP had paid a visit to Paragon two or three months ago. A reporter and photographer from the local paper had covered the occasion. It was possible later to buy copies of their photographs from the newspaper offices. She had bought some, among them one showing the MP with the Ansteys and their office staff, including Ian. 'I've got it back at the flat,' she told the Chief. When she left he had her driven home so she could hand over the photograph to the police driver.

After she had gone he leaned back in his chair. Something about Lilian Anstey that seemed to evoke resentment in other women. Not surprising, really. Clever, able, her share of looks, an elegant dresser, a settled position, no shortage of money; many women would envy that.

Bridget Farrell's face rose up before him, as he had last seen it, her expression alight with malice as she spoke of Lilian. Something else came back to him: the report on Lilian the Farrells had commissioned, and the name of the agent they had employed.

A phone call to the agent's address a few minutes later was answered by his wife. Her husband was away from home at present, working on a case. He wasn't expected back till around eleven tomorrow morning.

Kelsey chewed his lip. Could there possibly be anything in Delphine's flash of perception in the Paragon corridor – if such a moment had ever occurred? It might be no more than a piece of spiteful invention on Delphine's part, designed to take a little revenge on Ian Bryant for spurning her somewhat obvious charms.

But a person may be spiteful, he reflected, and still on occasion stumble upon the truth. It occurred to him as he stood up from his desk that one of the constables on the investigation team had a daughter working in the Paragon sales office; she might have an opinion on the subject of Miss Delphine Tate.

First thing next morning the Chief spoke to the constable who immediately went off home to catch his daughter before she set out on her Saturday shopping. He returned before long to say that his daughter had had quite a bit to say about Delphine.

She thought Delphine had a very high opinion of herself and in particular of her looks and charm. She was considered good at her work. She was generally acknowledged to have a bold and voracious sexual appetite. And yes, she was very capable of spite and malice, capable also of lying when it suited her.

At the press conference a little later the media hounds were in full cry. What had been behind the Chief's visit to Paragon, his address to the workforce? Had anything come of it? The questions came thick and fast. The Chief fielded them all with his customary skill, managing to avoid causing frustration and irritation while committing himself to little in the way of definite answers.

At eleven Lambert drove the Chief over to see the private inquiry agent hired by the Farrells. He proved willing to help but declared himself unable to hand over a copy of his report on Lilian Anstey, or even to give a verbal summary of its contents, without the express permission of the Farrells.

At the Chief's instigation he rang Bridget there and then. He caught her at home and put the question to her. She didn't need to think it over, she gave her answer at once and with pleasure: she had no objection whatever to a copy of the full report being made available to the police.

As soon as they got back to the station Kelsey shut himself away to read the report. He skimmed through the agent's account of how he had traced Lilian back to her beginnings, the contacts he had made, the places he had visited, the conversations he had held.

Lilian had, it seemed, been born in a village over towards the Welsh border. At the time of Lilian's birth her mother was in her late thirties and had been married for only a few months. She came from a humble background; she was a quiet, conscientious, hardworking woman with little in the way of looks. Her parents had died within a short time of each other when she was twenty, leaving her, their only child, their life savings. After their deaths she had gone on living in the rented cottage, travelling by bus every day to the nearby market town where she had worked as a sales assistant since leaving school. Her employer was the chief tobacconist and confectioner in the town; by the time of her marriage she had risen to the position of first saleswoman. She lived quietly and frugally, had little social life, saved a good deal of her salary.

She had been seduced by a travelling salesman by the name of Merrick who called regularly at the shop where she worked. When they married he moved into the cottage. A few weeks after Lilian's birth her mother went back to her job, leaving the baby in the care of a neighbour, a young married woman with a child of her own. Merrick continued as a travelling salesman.

He had told his wife he nursed ambitions for a business of his

144

own. Nothing would please him better than that they should run it together; he was sure they would make a success of it. When Lilian was two years old he announced that he had found a suitable business some distance away. It had been sadly neglected in recent years and was going for a knockdown price on the death of its elderly owner; it had undoubted possibilities. He persuaded his wife to turn over her savings.

A few weeks later an evening came when Merrick failed to return home as expected. His wife discovered that he had gone back to the cottage in the middle of the morning, had cleared out his belongings and driven off. She never again saw him or heard from him, never again saw one penny of her savings.

She took no steps in the matter but left it at that. She had no wish to advertise her gullibility to the world at large. She went on working; her neighbour continued to look after Lilian who went in due course with the neighbour's child to the village school.

In the winter when Lilian was nine years old her mother died of pneumonia following influenza. Lilian was put in a children's home in a nearby town, remaining there until she was sixteen. She was a quiet, industrious, well-behaved child; she did well at school. She had a particular flair for languages; she took a business course in her final year. On leaving school she soon found a job. She went into digs, continued to study at evening classes.

After a year or two she moved to a better job away from the area and continued in this pattern: studying, improving her qualifications, moving to better jobs. She never had, never wanted, a boyfriend.

When she was thirty she married her current boss, the owner of a small-scale business. He was a widower of sixty-five, apparently fit and healthy. Twelve months later he suffered an aneurysm which left him confined to a wheelchair. He lived on for another two years before suffering a massive stroke; he died in hospital twenty-four hours later.

From the start of his illness Lilian had run the business, with considerable success. He left her everything in his will. She had always been aware that he had a son by his first marriage. Father and son had never got on and the son had early taken up with dubious companions; he had subsequently led a wandering, disorderly existence. Nothing had been heard of him for years before his father remarried.

145

A week or two after the funeral the son had turned up. He was accompanied by his heavily pregnant girlfriend whom he had married the previous day. He claimed a right to the bulk of the inheritance for himself and his unborn child; he threatened court action.

He had no interest whatever in running the business and no ability to run it, even if he had wished to. In the end an out-of-court settlement was arrived at. The business had to be sold to allow the estate to be divided between Lilian and the son.

Lilian left the area and shortly afterwards got herself a job at Paragon as personal assistant to Robert Anstey.

Immediately after lunch DC Slade, armed with blow-ups of the faces of both Ian Bryant and Lilian Anstey, taken from the photograph supplied by Delphine Tate, drove out of the police station forecourt, turning his car in the direction of Martleigh. As soon as he had left Cannonbridge behind he pulled into a quiet lay-by to consider his mission.

If I were Ian Bryant, he thought, and if I were conducting an affair with Lilian Anstey, how would I set about it? The first consideration on Lilian's part would surely be to avoid being found out, so meetings in or anywhere near Cannonbridge would be ruled out. Ian was probably living either in digs or a small flat; Lilian would scarcely feel comfortable about visiting him in such surroundings, where gossip might be easily provoked.

The ideal meeting-place would be one where neither was likely to be recognized, with a total absence of nosy neighbours. I'd arrange to meet her half-way between Martleigh and Cannonbridge, he decided. We'd drive out to some isolated spot, a clearing in a small stretch of woodland, maybe. I'd select three or four places to meet, three or four spots to drive out to, making use of each in turn. I think we'd both feel relaxed enough in those conditions, safe enough from prying eyes.

He hadn't a cat in hell's chance of discovering any spot they drove out to, but the meeting-places were a different matter, there was a fair chance of discovering at least one of those.

What meeting-place would I choose? he asked himself, answering almost at once: I'd go for small, quiet, out-of-the-way country pubs. He could make only the roughest of guesses at how many such hostelries there might be in the relevant area; the search could take a long time. He switched on his engine and pulled out.

At the seventh pub he called at he struck lucky. The landlady immediately recognized Lilian's face. 'Oh yes!' she exclaimed. 'She's been in here several times.' She thought back. 'The first time would be July, early August, somewhere round there. Then once a week after that – though she hasn't been in at all these last three weeks or so. A Saturday or Sunday, it would be, occasionally an evening during the week.'

Slade asked if she had been alone.

The landlady smiled. 'She always came in alone but she always met her boyfriend here. He was younger than her but she was a smart, attractive woman. Always very quiet, the pair of them. Never stayed long.' She gazed down at the second photograph Slade held out. 'Yes, that's him all right. Good-looking chap.' She glanced up at Slade. 'What have they been up to? Don't tell me the police have taken up divorce inquiry work.'

When Slade got back into his car he resisted the temptation to head straight back to Cannonbridge but set resolutely off on a further round of pubs. Four calls later he was rewarded by a similar success.

I dare say I could find another pub or two, he thought as he left the premises, but two results like these would surely satisfy the Chief.

And indeed they did, when he got back to the station. One thought immediately struck the Chief: if Anstey had indeed been murdered, it was no longer possible to rule Lilian out on the grounds that she had spent the entire evening in full view at the charity dinner. If she had an accomplice in the shape of Ian Bryant she would now be very definitely in the picture.

We've got to tread very carefully here, he told himself, we've got to be very, very sure of what we're doing, we could come an awful cropper. Lilian Anstey is a woman of standing in the town.

And the fact that a couple have an affair doesn't necessarily mean they would conspire to murder the lady's husband.

Another thought sent the hair prickling along his scalp: the phone call from Kincraig to Stephen Hibberd that Friday

147

evening, the call he had accepted all along at its face value, the call that had helped to shore up the notion of suicide, what if that call had not been what it seemed?

Too late this evening to make a start on that but first thing tomorrow morning Slade would be on his way to sniff out any possible connection between Hibberd and Ian Bryant – or between Hibberd and Lilian Anstey.

As for himself, a visit to Miss Newsome in Devon might be no bad thing.

Slade set off next morning for the town where Ian Bryant had been at school. He would make his first call at the local police station to see if they could help him contact some retired teacher, living locally, who had taught at the school in Bryant's day.

But in the event he didn't need to talk to any retired teacher; one of the constables on duty turned out to have been a pupil at the school himself, in the same class as Bryant.

'I'm trying to discover,' Slade told him, 'if Bryant ever had any connection with someone by the name of Hibberd.'

'Stephen Hibberd?' the constable shot back. 'I'll say there was a connection! Stephen was in the same class, they lived in the same street. They were best mates all through school.'

24

'Do you know if they kept up with each other after school?' Slade asked.

The constable shook his head. 'That I couldn't say. Ian got a job elsewhere, I don't know what became of him. I could imagine he'd do quite well, he was clever enough and he always had an eye for the main chance. Stephen married a girl from school, she was in the class below us. Nell, her name was, a nice, sensible girl. Stephen has a woodturning business not far from here.

'Nell never liked Ian Bryant, she never trusted him. Ian could always turn on the charm when it suited him but Nell was always wary of him. Ian could do no wrong in Stephen's eyes.

Stephen was brought up in a children's home, he didn't have any family. He was a quiet lad, very hardworking but not very big or strong. He was bullied at school until Ian took him under his wing.'

He stared back into the old days. 'Ian didn't have much of a family himself. His mother died when he was seven or eight. His father was a lot older than the mother. He smoked like a chimney, you never saw him without a cigarette. His lungs packed up, he died just before Ian left school. Ian took off a few weeks later.'

When Slade left the police station he drove out to take a look at the woodturning premises, idle now on Sunday morning. They seemed well maintained, the windows recently washed, the surrounding area clean and tidy.

He made his way to the nearest pub, a cheerful place with a welcoming host and a friendly atmosphere; it was easy to get chatting with a group at the bar. He discovered before long that one of the men in the group worked for Stephen Hibberd.

'I should think you're doing all right these days,' Slade remarked casually. 'Business seems to be picking up all round.'

The man grimaced. 'We're all right now. But it was touch and go, a short time back. I was sure I was looking at the dole queue. Then we landed a contract with Paragon.' He grinned. 'Manna from heaven, I can tell you. Just about saved our bacon.'

Miss Newsome had retired to a small flat in a purpose-built block overlooking the promenade in her chosen resort. 'Suits me fine,' she told the Chief. 'Everything up-to-date, easy to keep clean. I can whisk round it in five minutes and have it looking shipshape.' She seemed full of bounding energy. 'I had to go out and find myself a little job,' she confided. 'After I'd settled in and got everything straight, got to know folk, taken a few trips, I was bored to tears.' She grinned. 'But I'm fine now. I've got a lovely little part-time job looking after a retired headmaster. He's a widower, nearly eighty, a very nice old man.'

'I wonder you retired so early,' Kelsey commented.

She jerked her shoulders. 'It wasn't my idea. I was perfectly happy at Kincraig. I had it in my head I'd soldier on there for another five years, at least.'

149

'You got on well with Mrs Anstey?'

She gave a decisive nod. 'Like a house on fire. Lovely lady. Very good at business, too, I understand. I reckon Mr Anstey fell on his feet there. I was very happy working for her. I was at Kincraig for the best part of four years after she married Mr Anstey and we never had a cross word. I was very fond of the first wife, too, she was a sweet lady, very kind. It was an awful blow to Mr Anstey when she took ill and died. I was pretty well in full charge of the household all the years after that, till he married again. It was very straightforward, working for him. He was very particular, a real stickler in every respect, but you always knew where you stood with him, you knew exactly what was required of you. If you did that, then there was never the slightest trouble. If he said supper at seven, he meant seven on the dot. That suited me down to the ground. I like order and regularity and punctuality myself, they're what keep the wheels turning.'

'How exactly did you come to retire?' Kelsey asked.

'I had my sixtieth birthday,' she told him, 'and Mr and Mrs Anstey made quite a fuss of me over that. They gave me some lovely presents and Mrs Anstey said I'd worked so hard for so long, it was time to take it easy, enjoy the rest of my life. They were going to give me a good pension – and I must say it's a very handsome one, a good deal more than I ever dreamed of – and a generous lump sum, as well. I was completely bowled over. I'd always liked this part of the coast, always thought I'd like to retire here one day, but it took me by surprise, coming just then, years before I ever thought it would happen. But what could I say? It did seem a very attractive idea.'

'When exactly was this?' Kelsey inquired.

'The end of June. They sent me off on a week's holiday – paid for by them – to look for somewhere to live. I found this flat right away. It was standing empty and the sale went through very quickly. Mrs Anstey found herself a daily housekeeper. She said they didn't fancy a stranger living in the house after me being there for so long, no one could ever take my place.' She smiled with reminiscent pleasure. 'They looked on me as one of the family, as you might say.'

'Did you ever see signs of bad temper in Mr Anstey?' Kelsey asked.

She looked astounded. 'Good heavens, no! Far from it! He was a very considerate, patient man, very good-hearted.'

At no time did she ask precisely why the Chief had called to see her. She appeared to accept the notion that detailed inquiries would be necessary in all cases of suicide. And she was in no doubt that Robert Anstey had taken his own life; she felt she could understand his reasons for doing so. 'He was a man of strong character, he wouldn't see any point in putting up with all that suffering when he was never going to get better. He'd want to spare his wife the worry and strain, the years of nursing, years of being tied.' She inclined her head. 'You've got to admire a man like that. It takes guts to do what he did.'

Had she ever come across a young man by the name of Ian Bryant while she was at Kincraig?

'Oh yes,' she replied at once. 'I remember him well. A very nice young man, beautiful manners. He came to the house quite a few times while I was there. He had a temporary job at Paragon. Mr Anstey told me how he'd come to take him on: some young tearaways were playing him up while he was driving his car and Ian came along and got rid of them for him. He came to supper sometimes or for lunch on a Sunday. Mr Anstey thought a lot of him. He told me Ian's parents were both dead. I think he almost looked on him as a son.'

DC Slade had been back in Cannonbridge for some time when the Chief returned from Devon. As soon as he heard what Slade had to tell him he set off with Lambert to talk to Stephen Hibberd.

When they reached the house they got no answer to Lambert's ring on the bell. A cheerful, chatty young woman came out of the next-door semi to say Stephen had driven his mother-in-law, Mrs Vine, his wife and their two children to pay a visit to Mrs Vine's old mother, living now with another daughter some sixty miles away; she didn't know the address. Mrs Vine and the two children would be spending a week there; Stephen and Nell would stay overnight before returning home tomorrow. They would be driving down again next Sunday to collect Mrs Vine and the children.

151

Did she know at what time the Hibberds would be returning home tomorrow?

'They should be here around seven thirty, seven forty-five,' she told them. 'Stephen will be dropping Nell off here and then going straight on to work. She'll go along there later.'

Light showed in a downstairs room when Lambert drew up before the Hibberds' house at seven forty-five on Monday morning.

Nell Hibberd answered their ring; she had got back a few minutes earlier. She didn't appear particularly surprised but stood looking out at them in uneasy silence.

'I realize this is an awkward moment to call,' Kelsey said. 'We'd be glad of a few minutes of your time, if we might come in.'

Still she said nothing but held the door back for them to enter, her face full of foreboding.

In the living-room Kelsey said: 'I won't waste your time and I hope you won't waste ours. We're here to find out the truth about the phone call we spoke to you about, three weeks ago. There are some aspects of the case concerning Mr Anstey's death that have come to the fore since we last spoke, one or two facts we know now that we didn't know then.' He ticked them off on his fingers. 'One: your woodturning business was saved from bankruptcy by the Paragon contract. Two: it is possible Robert Anstey's death was not suicide but murder set up to look like suicide.' Nell put both hands up to her face and sat crouching forward in her chair. 'Three,' Kelsey continued, 'a man by the name of Ian Bryant was employed for a time at Paragon and got on to a friendly footing with both the Ansteys. If Anstey's death was murder, there is some reason to suppose Bryant may have had a hand in it.' She sat rigidly motionless. 'Four,' Kelsey went on, 'we believe you and your husband have known Bryant from your schooldays.'

There was a brief silence. 'We want the truth,' Kelsey said. 'Who made that phone call to your husband? And what part did Bryant play in getting your business the Paragon contract?'

The silence lengthened. Out in the road the Monday-morning traffic went by.

152

At last she dropped her hands, raised her head and sat up. Her face was flushed, her eyes dull and heavy. She didn't speak, didn't meet the Chief's gaze.

Kelsey continued on a relentless note: 'There is some reason to believe a young boy, Billy Coleman, may have been killed in Anstey's house that night. He may have seen something, heard something, he may have got in the way.'

She began to utter little gasping sounds, her face grew very pale.

'You have children yourself,' Kelsey said. 'We believe you may be able to shed some light on what happened that night.'

She looked up at him now. Tears ran down her cheeks. 'Stephen didn't have any hand in either of those deaths,' she said in tones of great earnestness. 'Ian just made use of him. I didn't know anything about it at the time. I thought Mr Anstey really had decided to give us the contract, I thought he really did ring that evening.'

Her words came tumbling out. 'When you told us Mr Anstey had died, that he had an incurable illness, we really did both believe it was suicide. We read about Billy Coleman's murder but it never crossed our minds that it could have had anything to do with Mr Anstey's death. Then last Friday we heard on the local radio that you'd been to Paragon, you'd said there might be some link between the two deaths. Stephen looked dreadful when he heard that. I could see he was terribly worried about something but he wouldn't say what it was. He went out straight after he heard that piece on the radio, he wouldn't say where he was going. When he came back I kept on at him to tell me what was the matter. I wouldn't stop, I was determined to find out and in the end he broke down and told me.'

She continued her outpouring. When she had finished, Kelsey dispatched Lambert over to the works, to fetch her husband home. In the interval before they returned Kelsey made no further attempt to question Nell, nor did she show any wish to go on talking. She seemed to have said all it was in her to say. She lay back in her chair with her eyes closed, her hands lying loosely in her lap, doing her best, it appeared, to recover composure.

Kelsey stationed himself by the window overlooking the front garden and the road. It wasn't long before he saw the car draw up. Lambert and Stephen got out and came up the path. Stephen caught sight of the Chief standing at the window. Their eyes met. Stephen's face was creased in anxiety, his eyes tortured. Kelsey turned from the window and went out into the hall. Nell shifted in her chair, sat up, smoothed her clothes, patted her hair.

Stephen came into the room with Kelsey and Lambert. His eyes went to his wife, they exchanged anguished glances.

'You must understand,' Kelsey said to Stephen when they were all seated, 'that we're in possession now of a certain amount of the truth about what happened that night at Kincraig. We have some idea of the part you may have played in it. It's up to you how much more you intend to tell us now, but I can't see that holding back is going to do you any good in the long run. The whole truth has a way of coming out in the end.'

'Tell him everything you know,' Nell urged. She leaned forward, her face puckered in appeal.

Stephen lowered his head and sat staring down at the carpet. No one spoke or stirred. At last he looked up.

'All right,' he said to Kelsey in a tone stripped of expression. 'I don't know the whole of it by a long chalk but I'll tell you what I do know. We've no chance now of hanging on to the contract, anyway.' He didn't have to think back or struggle for words, it all came out pat, as if he had been over it countless times in his mind during long sleepless nights.

'Ian was working at Paragon when I went over to see Mr Anstey about getting on to the suppliers' list,' he said in the same dry, unemotional voice. 'I didn't know he was working there. We'd seen nothing of each other since we left school. I'd no idea what had become of him. He happened to catch sight of me that day, as I was leaving Paragon, he saw the name and address on the side of the van.' A few weeks later Ian had turned up at the works, wanting to put a proposition to him. He drove Stephen out to a quiet lay-by where they could talk in private.

He proposed that Stephen should be willing to accept a phone call from Ian at his home, at a date and time to be specified later. All he had to do was lift the receiver, exchange a word or two of mutual identification, remain on his end of the phone while Ian left his end, speak a final word when Ian returned a matter of minutes later, and then hang up. After that he must hold himself ready for a visit from the police, probably within the next day or two, during which he would be questioned about the call. What he would tell them would be exactly what Ian would instruct him to tell them – this would be disclosed to him if and when he decided to agree to the proposition. In due course it might, only might, be necessary for him to appear in court and repeat what he had told the police about the nature of the phone call. And that was it, the whole of it; nothing more would ever be required of him.

In return he would be guaranteed the contract he wanted with Paragon. It would be promptly and properly drawn up after the phone call and would last for as long as Stephen wanted it to last.

There were two final stipulations: he must ask no questions, ever, and he must utter not one syllable of any of this to his wife or any other living soul.

Ian gave him twenty-four hours to think it over. At the end of the twenty-four hours he phoned Stephen at the works and was given his reply: Stephen agreed to the proposition. 'I hadn't the foggiest notion what was behind it all,' he told the Chief, 'and I didn't want to know. I shut all that kind of thought out of my mind. I was desperate for the contract.' Ian met him again in the lay-by a few days later, gave him date and time, schooled him in precisely what he would say to the police and later, if required, in court.

The evening of Friday, 25th October arrived. Stephen stationed himself by the phone at home, took the call at nine fifteen as arranged. A day or two later when questioned by the police he gave his replies exactly as instructed.

He had been genuinely shocked and astonished when they told him of Anstey's death, but they also told him of Anstey's illness. It seemed to be generally believed that Anstey had committed suicide. He resolutely accepted that himself, he refused to allow his mind to dwell for an instant on any other possibility, to try to explore the part the phone call might have played in any of it.

The contract duly went through. He felt immense relief, settled down to working harder than ever at his business, thrust the whole affair out of his thoughts.

When he heard on the local radio that the inquest on Robert Anstey had again been adjourned, anxiety began to force its way up into his brain; he fought to subdue it.

Then last Friday evening he learned, again via local radio, of the Chief's visit to Paragon, his address to the workforce, the suggestion of a possible link between Anstey's death and the murder of Billy Coleman. He was knocked sideways, forced into the realization that he had got himself mixed up in something extremely nasty, though he still couldn't make out exactly what it could have been.

He left the house at once, drove to a call box and rang Ian's Martleigh flat. When Ian answered Stephen told him he was coming over right away, he wanted some explanations. Ian told him not to come to the flat, he'd meet him half-way, in a lay-by.

When Stephen got there Ian told him he was worrying himself over nothing. He refused to explain what lay behind the business of the phone call but swore he had had nothing whatever to do with the deaths of either Anstey or Billy Coleman, and what was more, he could prove it. He could say exactly where he was for every minute of that evening. He had been at a folk evening in a pub a few miles from Cannonbridge. The evening was a regular event; he had started attending when he worked at Paragon and had continued going there after moving to Martleigh.

He had spent the entire evening at the pub, arriving at around six forty-five and leaving at around eleven; at the end he had given a lift home to a couple of acquaintances, two young men who lived some ten miles away and had hitched a lift to the pub. He had dropped first one and then the other and then driven straight back to his flat, arriving there at around twelve thirty. He wrote down the names and addresses of the two acquaintances and pressed the slip of paper on Stephen, urging him to go and question the young men if he was still in any doubt.

'And did you question them?' Kelsey wanted to know.

Stephen shook his head. 'No, I didn't. When he gave me the names and addresses without being asked I reckoned it must be OK, he must have spent the evening the way he said he had. I couldn't see how he could possibly have had a hand in either of the murders – assuming Mr Anstey's death was also a murder, that is. I'd read that the police believed Billy's body had lain in one place for quite a time, and then been taken out to Crowswood. I couldn't see how Ian could possibly have been involved in that, there just wouldn't have been the time. So I made up my mind to put it all out of my head again.'

He glanced across at his wife. 'Nell could see there was something very wrong and in the end she got it out of me. I told her everything. She couldn't make head or tail of what had happened, any more than I could, but she did agree that Ian appeared to be fully accounted for that evening. In the end we decided we'd better keep our mouths shut and try to forget the whole thing.'

25

As soon as Kelsey got back to the station he sent DC Slade off to the two addresses Ian Bryant had given Stephen Hibberd, to check Ian's account of that Friday evening. He also dispatched officers over to Martleigh, to the firm where Ian worked, with instructions to bring him in, together with his car. If he refused to come voluntarily then he was to be arrested.

But Ian didn't refuse. He registered surprise and a certain amount of protest, but no more. He declared himself unable to imagine why the police should want to talk to him but if there was any way he could be of assistance, then he was willing to give what help he could.

His manner was certainly in no way downcast or subdued when he arrived at the station. Kelsey made himself known and the process of interviewing began. Ian didn't demand a solicitor. When the matter was raised he showed momentary surprise – he had done nothing wrong, he saw no reason for a solicitor, he was happy to answer any questions put to him.

Kelsey began by asking for his movements during the evening of Friday, 25th October. Easy enough to remember, Ian told him: he had spent the evening at a pub a mile or two outside Cannonbridge. He then went on to repeat more or less what they had already been told of his movements via Stephen Hibberd.

Had Ian set foot in Kincraig at any time in the course of that evening?

No, he most certainly had not. He had not been anywhere near Kincraig.

Did he make a phone call from Kincraig that evening?

He shook his head with vigour. Certainly not.

Kelsey switched tack. 'Are you acquainted with a man by the name of Stephen Hibberd?'

Ian nodded. 'I was at school with him.'

'When did you last have any kind of contact with him?'

He moved his head. 'I can't recall exactly. It was years ago. I don't think I ever saw him after we left school and I moved away.'

'Did you phone Hibbered from Kincraig on the evening of 25th October?'

He looked surprised. 'I certainly did not.'

Kelsey executed another change of tack. 'What is your relationship with Mrs Lilian Anstey?'

He showed mild surprise but answered readily: 'I knew her when I worked at Paragon Tools. I was there for a time in the summer. I came into contact with her sometimes in the course of my duties but it was mainly Mr Anstey I worked for. He asked me over to Kincraig a few times for a meal.'

'Was there ever any relationship of a more personal nature with Mrs Anstey?'

Again a vigorous headshake. 'Certainly not. She was the boss's wife. Ten years older than me.'

'When did you last have any kind of contact with her?'

'I haven't had any contact with her since I left Paragon back in October – 11th October, if I remember rightly.'

Kelsey swept straight on. 'We have good reason to believe you met Mrs Anstey on several occasions away from Paragon, both during the time you worked there and after you left.'

'That's absolute rubbish!' he retorted. 'I've never laid eyes on her since I left Paragon.'

'We have very sound witnesses to say otherwise. To say you met the lady two or three times a week in quiet pubs, both during much of the time you worked at Paragon and after you left.'

There was a brief silence. Ian didn't appear in the least abashed. He smiled slightly. 'Maybe we did have something going there for a while.' He gestured airily. 'You know how it is. A good-looking woman, older husband, likes to kick up her heels once in a way. No real harm in it. But it's over now, it's been over some time.'

'What ended it?'

'It came to an end when I left Paragon. Lilian had been told about her husband's illness. That killed it stone dead. She wanted to look after him, be with him more in the evenings and at weekends.' He gave the Chief a direct look. 'She was really very fond of him. I was just a bit on the side.' He moved his shoulders. 'I was glad, in a way. I'd got to like and respect Anstey, he'd been good to me. I wasn't feeling too comfortable about having it off with his wife.'

'We know you met her after you left Paragon.'

He pulled down the corners of his mouth. "Maybe once or twice. You know how it is with some women, particularly older women. They make up their minds to end it but they can't let go right away. I did meet her a couple of times, just to persuade her it really was all over, it was best that way. She accepted it in the end and that was that."

'Did Mrs Anstey know you paid a visit to Kincraig that Friday evening, 25th October?'

He shot back at once: 'I never set foot in Kincraig that evening.'

'We have very good reason to believe you made a phone call from Kincraig that evening to Stephen Hibberd at his home. He is prepared to stand up in court and swear to that.'

'I made no such phone call,' Ian snapped back. 'Whatever reasons Hibberd may have for saying I did.'

'Did you approach Hibberd a few weeks ago? Did you put a proposition to him?' He outlined the proposal Hibberd had spoken of.

'That's a load of sheer codswallop,' Ian retorted briskly. 'I can only think Stephen must be having some sort of nervous breakdown. Nothing like that in any way at all ever took place. I never got in touch with him, never went to see him, never met him in any lay-by, never made him any sort of proposal. I haven't set eyes on him for years.'

'But Hibberd's contract did go through,' Kelsey pointed out.

'What on earth has that got to do with me?' Ian demanded with heat. 'I know nothing about any contract. I left Paragon weeks ago. I know nothing about Stephen's business or what he may have been up to or why he's trying to drag me into something I know nothing about.'

Kelsey terminated the interview a little later, informing Ian that there would now be an interval for rest and refreshment before the interview was resumed. Ian's manner was still confident and assertive, he remained totally unshaken.

DC Slade tracked down without difficulty the two young men Ian Bryant had named; both readily confirmed what Ian had told the police about his movements that Friday evening. They were not, it seemed, close friends of Ian, they merely knew him casually through occasional meetings at the folk evenings.

Slade drove next to Martleigh, to the converted Edwardian house where Ian rented the first-floor flat; there were two other flats in the house. No one answered Slade's ring at the ground-floor flat but a middle-aged housewife came to the door of the top flat. She proved of little help; she was unable to recall that evening with any certainty and had no idea now, if she had ever known, what time Ian Bryant had returned home. She told Slade the ground-floor flat was rented by a young couple. The husband was a travelling salesman, always away during the week, but the wife could be reached at the office in town where she worked. Slade went to the office and managed a word with her. She had no special recollection of that Friday evening, she was unable to say at what time Ian had come home.

Not a very successful mission, Slade reflected with some irritation as he returned to his car. He switched on his engine and was about to drive off, back to Cannonbridge, when he changed his mind and turned the car once more in the direction of Ian Bryant's flat.

When he reached Martleigh he called at the properties on either side of the house where Ian lived, asking such residents as he came across if they had any knowledge of Ian's movements that Friday night; he covered half-a-dozen properties with no success whatever. He crossed the road and began working his way in a similar fashion through the houses opposite.

His visits to the first four houses proved fruitless but his mood remained one of stubborn persistence as he opened the gate of the fifth property, a tall house divided into four flats. He got no answer to his rings at the first three flats but undeterred he climbed the last flight of stairs and set his finger on the fourth bell.

He was rewarded by shuffling sounds within and a minute later the door opened an inch or two on a chain and a suspicious eye peered out. Slade identified himself and was reluctantly admitted by an elderly man whose manner livened up considerably as Slade's questioning took him back to that Friday evening, which he remembered with a reminiscent shudder.

He had not the slightest difficulty in recalling that evening, it had been a highly unpleasant one as far as he was concerned. He had had one of his few remaining teeth extracted a few days earlier and an infection had arisen in the socket. He had woken on the Friday morning to find his cheek swollen, discoloured and throbbing. He managed to get an emergency appointment with his dentist who prescribed an antibiotic to be taken every four hours. He was warned not to take any painkiller in conjunction with the antibiotic, however much he might be tempted; he should begin to find some alleviation of the discomfort within twenty-four hours or so.

He spent a very uncomfortable evening. He went to bed at midnight but was unable to sleep. His next dose of medicine wasn't due till 2 a.m. At one thirty, unable to endure the tossing and turning any longer, he got out of bed, put on his slippers and dressing-gown, and went along to the kitchen to make himself a hot drink. He carried it back to his bedroom, drew back a curtain and switched off the light. He stood by the window, sipping his drink, looking out at the night, waiting for the minutes to tick by.

At one fifty he saw Bryant's car turn into the driveway opposite. He knew the car; he had spoken to Bryant three or four times. Yes, he was quite certain of the time. Ten minutes later he was able to take his next dose of medicine. He got back into bed, thankfully falling asleep at last a little later.

On the way back to Cannonbridge Slade stopped at the pub Ian had named. The landlord told him the folk evenings were always very well attended; there was always an overflow into the large garden. When Slade took a look round the premises he saw how easy it would be for someone attending the folk evening to slip away unnoticed for a time and return equally unnoticed later.

161

He made good time back to the station and was able to speak to the Chief before the questioning of Ian Bryant was resumed. Kelsey listened intently and then went back to the interview room.

He began by getting Ian to repeat that he had had no contact of any kind with Lilian Anstey after the two brief meetings when he had finally persuaded her to accept that the affair was over. Would Ian swear in court there had been no further contact? Yes, he most certainly would.

Kelsey next got him to repeat his timings for the evening of Friday, 25th October, concluding with the fact that he had arrived back at his flat around twelve thirty and gone straight to bed. Again he asked if Ian would be prepared to swear to those timings in court. Yes, he would indeed be prepared.

'We have good reason,' Kelsey told him, 'to believe you arrived back at your flat a good deal later than twelve thirty. We have an excellent witness ready to swear that you arrived home at one fifty. A gap of one hour and twenty minutes. Where were you during that time? It was long enough for you to cover quite some distance in a car. Driving out, maybe, after you'd dropped the second of the two young men, to Crowswood, and then, finally, back to Martleigh.'

'I was nowhere near Crowswood,' Ian threw back at him. 'That night or any other night. I never had any reason to go to Crowswood. Your witness is either mistaken or lying, he's certainly not telling the truth.'

'You have no real alibi for the earlier part of that evening,' Kelsey pointed out. 'You would have had no difficulty at all slipping away from the pub to pay a visit to Kincraig.'

'I tell you again,' Ian retorted, 'I never left the pub till the end. I never set foot in Kincraig.'

Kelsey regarded him. 'You got on to intimate terms with Lilian Anstey. Maybe at first it was never intended on either side to be anything more than a passing affair but then you learned of Anstey's illness. That completely altered your attitude. You began to think maybe Anstey wouldn't last all that much longer. Nothing to stop you, after his death, marrying his widow, moving into Kincraig, setting yourself up as joint owner of Paragon.'

Ian made no response except to thrust out a hand in a

forcefully dismissive gesture. He wore a look of patience being tried beyond reasonable limits.

Kelsey went on: 'But then you learned that Anstey might live for many years. You didn't feel inclined to wait that long. It occurred to you that maybe there was no need to wait for Anstey's death, you might perhaps help to bring it forward. You gave the matter some thought, you gave it a very great deal of thought. The notion of suicide floated up. Folk would probably be ready to accept the death of an incurably ill man as suicide, provided all the circumstances, all the details of the death were right, the whole thing planned every inch of the way, carefully executed.' He leaned forward. 'And that's the very situation we have now. Robert Anstey is dead. His death is generally accepted as suicide. There's nothing whatever to stop you, after a decent interval, marrying his widow.'

Ian uttered a sound of derisive contempt.

'Did you talk Lilian into it bit by bit?' Kelsey asked. 'Did you persuade her it would save her husband years of suffering? And it would save her years of nursing, dancing attendance on an increasingly helpless man, waiting for her inheritance? Did you make her see she could get it all now, while she was still young enough to enjoy having a young husband to share it with?'

Ian said not a word but looked grimly back at him with an air of dissociating himself from the nonsense that was being aired.

'I put it to you,' Kelsey pursued, 'that once you'd got Lilian to agree to it you planned it all between you, down to the very last detail. The article in the Sunday magazine gave you the method. That was it, you both decided: foolproof. When the time came you carried it all out exactly as you had planned. It all went like clockwork till it came to the moment when you were to return to Anstey's study to speak a word to Hibberd waiting on the other end of the phone. Then it was a matter of replacing the receiver, leaving, driving back to the pub, mingling with the crowd for the rest of the evening.

'But that was the moment when things went wrong, when something happened you hadn't planned for. You replaced the receiver, you turned to leave the study. And then, behind the curtain, you heard someone sneeze.'

A hush fell over the room.

The Chief went on: 'You crossed the room and pulled back the curtain. You saw a small boy staring up at you in fright. You dealt with him on the instant. You found something to wrap the body. You carried the body out to the car, you locked it away in the boot. You drove back to the pub. You stayed to the end of the evening. You looked about for someone to offer a lift to, to strengthen your alibi. You dropped the two young men off. You headed out for some lonely spot where you could dump the body. You got to Crowswood, you took the body from the boot, removed the wrapping, to be disposed of later. You carried the body down the slope, concealing it as best you could. You went back up the slope, got into your car and returned to your flat.

'Early next morning, when you were sure Lilian would be alone in the house, you rang to tell her about the boy. You told her to sit tight, keep her nerve, everything would be all right.

'Did you tell her you'd better not meet for the present? You'd keep in touch by phone and only by phone, nothing in writing, ever?'

Ian leaned forward. 'You think yourself very clever. You think you can keep on at me, you can bully me, put pressure on me and I'll crack, I'll sign anything you want me to sign. You're desperate for a result on Billy Coleman's murder, you've decided I'll fit the bill.' He struck the table with his fist. 'I'm here to tell you you've picked the wrong man, I don't break that easily. I'm not going to sit here and let you stitch me up for something I didn't do, something I know nothing about. Lilian warned me you'd try every trick in the book.'

There was a moment's electric silence. Kelsey's heart began to pound. 'And when was that?' he demanded. 'When exactly did Lilian warn you? You told us just now you had no contact of any kind with her for some weeks.'

Ian had got a grip on himself again. 'I had to ring her, naturally, when I heard of Robert's death.'

'And when exactly was that?'

'I heard it on the local radio on the Saturday morning. I rang her then.'

'Why did you ring her?'

'To say how very sorry I was to hear that Robert had taken his own life. To offer my deepest sympathy.'

'Those first radio broadcasts that Saturday morning made no

164

mention whatever of suicide, they said nothing about the manner of death, they simply said Robert Anstey had been found dead in his house.' He directed at Ian a piercing gaze. 'You're telling me Lilian's instant response when you rang to offer your sympathy was to say: "Watch out! The police will try to trick you into admitting you murdered Robert. Don't let them pin it on you!"'

Silence fell again over the room; it deepened, lengthened.

'I think you'd better start talking,' Kelsey said into the silence.

26

Ian sat motionless, his eyes closed. At last he opened his eyes.

'Yes, I think perhaps I should,' he said calmly. 'I'm not going to let her pin it all on me. It was never my idea. It was her idea from the start. She did all the persuading, not me. If I'm going down for it I'll make sure I take her with me. She didn't want Robert living for another twenty years, getting worse every day. She talked me into it. She kept on at me, she got me into a state where I'd do anything she asked.'

And talk he did, a voluble outpouring, under caution, though he still didn't want a solicitor. He described the plan, its execution, every last detail of it, he insisted, worked out by Lilian, not by him. She had left the back door unsecured, securing it again herself later. She had put everything ready for him, instructed him where everything would be found, instructed him about the scarf, the magazine cutting, the switching of the contaminated items from the bedside tray, from the kitchen, replacing them with clean items. She was the brains, the prime mover, he was merely the besotted fool who had put the plan into operation.

He spoke of Billy Coleman's death without any shred of emotion or remorse, with a kind of irritated censure. The death, he asserted, had been the purest accident, never intended. It had been forced on him, Billy had only himself to blame. If he hadn't sneaked into the house in the first place, looking for what he could find, it would never have happened.

He had snatched up a silk wrap from Lilian's bedroom, to carry the body out to his car; he had burned the wrap later.

He glanced up at the clock. 'She'll know the game's up by now. She'll have tried to ring me at work. They'll have told her the police came for me.' They had taken it in turns to ring each other twice a day, between 11.15 a.m. and 11.30 a.m., and between 8 p.m. and 8.15 p.m. Just a word or two to say everything was OK, no problems. If there was no call within the prescribed fifteen minues, that signalled trouble. Today it had been Lilian's turn to ring.

When DC Slade got to Paragon Lilian was no longer there. She was, he was told, due to attend a business lunch, an annual function of some importance, being held in the town's largest hotel. Guests would assemble at twelve forty-five; lunch would be served at 1 p.m.

Lilian had, it appeared, left Paragon shortly after eleven thirty, telling her secretary she had a couple of calls to make before the lunch.

Slade drove at once to Kincraig where Hester Whiting answered the door. No, Mrs Anstey was not in the house. She hadn't returned there in the course of the morning, nor had she phoned.

Slade asked Hester if she would ring the police station immediately if Mrs Anstey should return or phone, without, if at all possible, alerting Mrs Anstey to the fact that she was making the call.

Hester gazed at him for several moments before replying. Her face was set like stone. She asked no questions and Slade offered no explanations. At last she told him yes, she would do as he asked.

Would she also agree to remain at Kincraig for the time being, not go off for her usual afternoon break? Yes, she would remain. He told her they would be in touch with her again shortly and drove back to the hotel where the first guests were now arriving. Mrs Anstey was not, it seemed, amongst them.

The minutes ticked by. More guests arrived. One o'clock came. The meal got under way. Over the next ten minutes a few latecomers came hurrying in and slipped into the dining-room to take their places. Still no sign of Lilian.

At one twenty Slade left the hotel, returning briefly to the police station to report to the Chief, leaving immediately afterwards for Paragon where he spoke again to Lilian's secretary. No, there had been no sign of Mrs Anstey, no word from her. Yes, she would phone the police station the moment Mrs Anstey came in or rang.

When the early edition of the local evening paper appeared on the news-stands it carried a couple of stop-press paragraphs referring to Ian Bryant being taken in for questioning. Reporters were by now gathering in force outside the police station.

Shortly after three thirty Forensic were able to give the Chief the results of their scrutiny of Ian's car: they had found grey silk fibres in two places in the boot of the car: caught up on the head of a screw and on a roughened metal edge. The fibres were identical with those discovered on the clothing on Billy Coleman's body.

At four fifteen Ian Michael Bryant was charged with the murders of Robert James Anstey and William Edward Coleman. He would be brought before the magistrates in the morning for the formal charge. The information was given to the press waiting outside the station and went out shortly afterwards over local radio, together with an appeal for Mrs Lilian Anstey to contact the police without delay.

A little later Sergeant Lambert drove the Chief round to Kincraig. When Hester Whiting opened the door it was plain she had been crying. 'I heard the newsflash,' she said in shaking tones. There was still no sign of Mrs Anstey, no word from her. She asked no questions, offered no comment, no opinion.

When Kelsey inquired if she knew of any garment or article made of grey silk, she answered him at once, with the air of someone beginning to perceive a solution to some mystery. 'I'd forgotten that!' she exclaimed.

Mrs Anstey, it appeared, had owned a light wrap of fine grey silk which she often wore when dressing; Hester hadn't seen it for some time. In the course of her tidying around on the morning after Mr Anstey's death, she had picked up the narrow sash belt belonging to the wrap; it was lying on the carpet behind an easy chair in Mrs Anstey's bedroom. She had looked about for the wrap but couldn't see it. She had rolled up the belt and put it in a corner of one of the open shelves in the fitted wardrobe. In the turmoil of that day and the days that followed she hadn't given it another thought. She had never subsequently laid eyes on the grey wrap, nor had she ever mentioned the matter to Mrs Anstey.

She took the two policemen up to Lilian's bedroom and opened the wardrobe. In the corner of a shelf lay the belt, neatly rolled. Kelsey took possession of it.

On the way downstairs again she suddenly said: 'Something else I noticed, I'd forgotten it until now.' Under the regime adopted by Mr Anstey after his illness was diagnosed, she had prepared a bedtime tray for him every evening before going off duty. The milk beverage powder required only the addition of hot water, plus any sugar that might be wanted.

She always put out on the tray one of the large old breakfast cups and saucers Mr Anstey – and only Mr Anstey – always used. He was fond of the cups and saucers, part of a Victorian set belonging to the grandmother of his first wife. They had been in use in Kincraig since the day they were bought and there were now only three cups and saucers remaining.

When Hester first started working at Kincraig she noticed that one of the cups had a tiny chip on the underside of the handle. 'I'm fussy about things like that,' she explained. 'I like things just so, particularly things of quality.' She had made a point of never putting out the chipped cup for Mr Anstey. Two or three days after his death, when she was tidying the kitchen cupboard, she noticed that neither of the two cups remaining was chipped. The third cup, taken from the bedside tray on the night Mr Anstey died, had gone with its saucer and teaspoon to the forensic laboratory. That could only mean that the cup set out on Mr Anstey's tray that evening was the chipped cup.

'But I'm positive I didn't put the chipped cup out on the tray.' She stared earnestly up at the Chief. 'I'd wager my life on that.' No, she had said nothing about it to Mrs Anstey, it had seemed too trivial a matter for that. In the kitchen she showed Kelsey the two remaining cups; neither had any chip. It all squared, Kelsey reflected, with what Ian had told them about the switching of the items.

He asked if Mr Anstey had always used the same brand of milk beverage at bedtime.

'Oh no!' she replied at once. 'When I first came here neither of them took anything of the sort at bedtime.' After Mr Anstey was told about his illness and he started going to bed early with a hot drink, Mrs Anstey had bought him a chocolate-based beverage. 'Then later she bought him a different one. She said she'd read the labels and decided it was a better mixture, she thought it would give better sleep. Mr Anstey quite got to like it and he always had it after that. It wasn't as sweet as the first one so he always took plenty of sugar with it.'

A sprinkling of powdered sleeping-pills wouldn't show up on a white beverage mix as it would on a chocolate-based product, Kelsey reflected. A man of regular habits, Miss Newsome had said of Robert Anstey, a man for punctuality and order. He could surely be relied on to make his hot drink at precisely the same time every night. Easy enough for someone with murder in mind to work out by what time the doctored beverage would have sent Anstey into a profound sleep.

An interview with Chief Inspector Kelsey went out in the early-evening TV news, to be repeated in later news slots. Lilian Anstey's photograph appeared on the screen. The registration number of her car, its make and colour, were given, together with a description of the clothes she was wearing when last seen. Anyone with any information about the present whereabouts of Mrs Anstey was asked to contact the police, who were anxious to interview her in connection with the deaths of Robert Anstey and Billy Coleman. Similar statements went out over national and local radio.

Responses came in swiftly, among them two phone calls that seemed to Kelsey to stand out from the rest by virtue of the details they mentioned which had not been included in any of the broadcasts.

The first call came from the owner of a general store in a village some thirty miles away. He had watched the five forty TV news and felt certain Mrs Anstey's photograph was that of a woman who had called into his store half an hour earlier. He gave the make and colour of her car but hadn't noticed the registration number. He listed the purchases she had made, paying for them in cash. He was also able to give the direction in which she had driven off.

The second call was from an attendant at a petrol station-cum-store on the outskirts of a village some forty miles from the general store of the previous call. The pumps at the station were operated by the attendant. The woman had driven in a few minutes before six. She had bought petrol and a can of soft drink, she had paid in cash. He noticed that she seemed pre-occupied and would have left without her change had he not reminded her. He gave the make and colour of her car, but not the registration number. He gave also the direction she had taken on leaving.

After she left he watched the 6 p.m. news on TV. It struck him at once that the photograph of Mrs Anstey was very like the woman he had just seen.

Kelsey studied a map. I believe I know where she's heading, he thought. Fifteen minutes later DC Slade and another officer, thoroughly briefed, pulled out of the station forecourt and set off for the Welsh border.

The evening had turned cold and blustery by the time they reached their destination. They pulled up outside the village pub and Slade went in to talk to the landlord. He came out a few minutes later and got back into the car. They drove a little way out of the village, halting before a cottage set back from the road.

Light showed from a downstairs room at the back. It was a minute or two before the householder, an elderly man, answered their ring.

Yes, a woman had stopped her car outside the cottage earlier in the evening. He gazed down at the photograph Slade held out. Yes, it could be the same woman. She hadn't rung the bell, she had simply got out of the car and stood staring at the house.

He hadn't watched TV that evening, he had been doing a job in his workshop. He happened to be upstairs when he heard the car stop and glanced out. He didn't recognize the woman. When she remained looking at the house he thought perhaps she had lost her way. He went downstairs and opened the front door. She had scarcely seemed to be aware of him. It struck him that she was in some kind of trouble. He stepped outside and asked if she needed help.

She seemed to recollect herself. She thanked him, said she was all right, adding, in explanation: 'I lived here once, a long time ago.' She apologized for disturbing him, got back into her car and drove off. He hadn't noted the registration number but his recollection of the vehicle accorded well with Lilian's. He had stood at the door for a minute or two, watching her go, he had seen the direction she took; it led only to a stretch of woodland. He had wondered briefly if she had taken the wrong turning but then recalled her saying she had lived in the house, so presumably she knew the area, knew what she was doing.

As they reached the edge of the wood they heard the distant throb of an engine. They halted the car and jumped out. Slade snatched up a torch and a jack handle from the boot. They ran through the trees, led on by the sound to where the car stood in a little clearing. They saw the hose snaking in at the car window.

Lilian lay on her side on the rear seat with a hand under her cheek, a coat folded under her head, a white envelope by the fingers of her other hand.

They pulled her out on to the grass and Slade felt for the pulse in her neck. It was still feebly beating.

27

On the last day of the old year the consultant in charge of Lilian Anstey found a few minutes from his busy schedule to have a word with Chief Inspector Kelsey. After their talk, in the middle of the afternoon, the Chief came down the steps of the Cannonbridge General Hospital where Lilian was being treated as a private patient. She would shortly be transferred to a private hospital some miles away, under the ample financial provision made for her under Robert Anstey's will.

The Chief walked across to his car, mulling over what the consultant had told him. In the light of current medical knowledge Lilian was likely to remain in a persistent vegetative state. She might live on for many years, even into old age, with no prospect of any improvement. 'I doubt your men did her any favour by pulling her out of the car,' the consultant had said. 'Another few minutes and she would have slipped away for good.'

The Chief got into his car and headed for the police station. As he drove past the industrial estate he saw the lights of Paragon in full blaze. Under the terms of Anstey's will Bridget Farrell was now in control of the business as sole owner. She was forging ahead, absorbed in plans for the future; she appeared to command the support and confidence of the workforce. Keith Farrell had left his job with the estate agency and was now working at Paragon. The pair were apparently working well and harmoniously together though it was plain that it was Bridget who was in charge and intended to remain in charge.

Kelsey had a sudden vision of Lilian Anstey as she had been in the days before he had met her, when he had seen her at functions in the town: an elegant, handsome woman, intelligent and energetic. Another vision rose up before him, Lilian as he had just seen her, lying motionless in bed, with long, long, unvisited years ahead of her, unable to feel, to think, to understand, to communicate. He felt an icy shiver run along his spine. Not a fate he would wish on anyone.

Any future application to switch off her life-support machinery could only be made by Bridget Farrell, who was now Lilian's sole remaining connection of any kind. But as any trust funds remaining on Lilian's death would go to Bridget, no court would look with favour on such an application by her; the machinery would never be switched off.

Bridget had decided to honour the contract with Stephen Hibberd. He was supplying goods of high quality and impeccable finish at the keenest prices and she was certain his relief and gratitude at banishing the spectre of bankruptcy would ensure he would always be one of Paragon's most reliable suppliers.

It was unlikely that Stephen would be prosecuted for his part in the phone call set-up, in view of the subsequent wholehearted and valuable co-operation of both the Hibberds.

Nor was it likely that any prosecution for receiving stolen goods would be brought against Matthew Shardlow, in the absence of hard evidence against him.

172

Bridget Farrell would dearly have relished sacking Shardlow, challenging him to take Paragon to a tribunal, but she was too astute to go down that tempting path; she knew too much about the law and its vagaries, the uncertainty of outcome, the certainty of high costs; Paragon could pay dearly for such an exercise in self-indulgence. She had decided to take her solicitor's advice and pay Shardlow off. She was able to comfort herself with the thought that she was starting out at Paragon with a clean slate, unburdened by worrying litigation.

But on one point she was adamant: Shardlow would get no reference from Paragon. Without it he was unlikely ever to find another job. Kelsey could see him using his pay-off money to set himself up as a dealer. He might do very well at it – and would probably take care not to dabble in grey areas of the trade, knowing the certainty of a police eye being kept on him.

Bridget had put Kincraig up for sale and it had found a buyer almost at once. The Farrells had also put their own semi on the market and were now looking for something a little larger, within easy reach of Paragon. Bridget had suggested to Hester Whiting that she might like to work part-time for them when they had found their new house but Hester had declined the offer. 'I'll never take another domestic job,' she vowed to Kelsey. 'You get drawn into things.' She was only forty years old, by no means too old, she felt, to make something of herself, build up a positive and confident new life. On one thing she was resolutely determined: she would never again be in any way dependent on any man but would stand firmly on her own two feet. She intended to make a start by enrolling at the local college of further education for the new term and would first of all seek from them an assessment of her capabilities and potential.

Glenna Coleman had changed the colour of her hair, but her nature wouldn't allow her, even at this stage in her life, to settle for a subdued, unobtrusive tint; her locks were now a bright, gleaming chestnut. She had reverted to her maiden name and taken off for London, mightily relieved to be shaking off the dust of Cannonbridge from her feet. She had assured the Chief she would keep her local police station informed of her address; she would hold herself ready, if required, to give evidence at the trial.

When Ian Bryant was told how Lilian had been found, he

received the news with no sign of emotion. 'She should have made a better job of it,' was his only comment, but the Chief detected an underlying satisfaction that Lilian would not be there to deny one word of what he would have to say in court.

Lilian had left no letter for Ian, only the letter addressed to the Chief. In it she offered no excuses, no justification. She expressed neither remorse nor self-pity; she made no attempt to lay all the blame on Ian. She had written a clear outline of what had been planned and carried out, straightforward and businesslike; it accorded with what Ian had told them – except that she laid the blame squarely on both their shoulders.

Ian had, it appeared, decided it would serve him best in all the circumstances to plead guilty to both murders, shifting as much blame as possible on to Lilian, emphasizing his comparative youth and inexperience of life alongside Lilian's maturity, pleading what he intended to describe as his irresistible infatuation, her ruthless domination of him. The Chief took leave to doubt the truth and force of these protestations; he was strongly of the opinion that no British jury was likely to prove as gullible as Ian plainly hoped. He could see not the slightest chance of Ian escaping two life sentences.

Ian was, it appeared, keeping himself occupied in prison with a good deal of physical exercise – and in assiduously studying law, in which he now took a consuming interest. If he kept his nose clean and came out of prison in due course, he would still be a comparatively young man. He might well by then have equipped himself with an Open University degree in law – with what consequences, once he was a free man again, the Chief didn't care to contemplate.

He reached the police station and drove on to the forecourt. A breeze had sprung up and blew across his face with the smell of rain as he got out of his car.

Mustn't be late getting off this evening; he was spending it with old friends, seeing in the New Year.

And mustn't be too late, New Year's Eve or not, in getting to bed. Whatever the New Year might hold, tomorrow was another working day.